Evergreen Wishes at Moonglow

Evergreen Wishes at Moonglow

A Moonglow Christmas Novella

Deborah Garner

Cranberry Cove Press

Cranberry Cove Press

PO Box 1671

Jackson, WY 83001, United States

Cover design by Mariah Sinclair | www.mariahsinclair.com

Library of Congress Catalog-in-Publication Data Available

Garner, Deborah

Evergreen Wishes at Moonglow / Deborah Garner—1st United States edition
1. Fiction 2. Woman Authors 3. Holidays

p. cm.

ISBN-13

978-1-952140-26-6 (paperback)

978-1-952140-27-3 (hardback)

10 9 8 7 6 5 4 3 2

Books by Deborah Garner

The Paige MacKenzie Mystery Series
Above the Bridge
The Moonglow Café
Three Silver Doves
Hutchins Creek Cache
Crazy Fox Ranch
Sweet Sierra Gulch

The Moonglow Christmas Novella Series
Mistletoe at Moonglow
Silver Bells at Moonglow
Gingerbread at Moonglow
Nutcracker Sweets at Moonglow
Snowfall at Moonglow
Yuletide at Moonglow
Starlight at Moonglow
Joy at Moonglow
Evergreen Wishes at Moonglow

The Sadie Kramer Flair Series
A Flair for Chardonnay
A Flair for Drama
A Flair for Beignets
A Flair for Truffles
A Flair for Flip-Flops
A Flair for Goblins
A Flair for Shamrocks

Cranberry Bluff
Sweet Treats

For my mother,
who always made holidays special for us.

Chapter One

"WHAT WILL YOU WISH FOR, BETTY?"

Mist sat across the kitchen counter from Betty, her hands wrapped around a mug of peppermint tea, Betty's own around a mug of coffee. No morning was complete without visiting with the hotelkeeper, who'd become a mother figure to her over the years.

"I'm still deciding," Betty said, blowing across her coffee mug to cool it. "There are so many things to wish for."

Mist took a sip of tea and thought about the idea that had come about during a random discussion with Maisie while chatting at her floral boutique. The concept of hanging wishes on a Christmas tree had enchanted them immediately, and the townsfolk had jumped in with enthusiasm. Clayton, the town's fire chief and Maisie's husband, had found a tall evergreen in a thick pine forest not far from town. In true mountain fashion, he'd cut the tree down and brought it to town, where it now stood proudly in the center of the town park.

Betty inhaled the intoxicating smell of what Mist called

Java Love, brewed daily from a freshly ground mix of coffee beans. "Not just for myself but for others."

Mist nodded. "You could hang more than one if that's what your heart tells you. Marge ordered cases of those clear ornaments, plenty for multiple wishes."

Those had been a welcome discovery, round plastic ornaments that could be filled and then closed, keeping the contents safe from the weather. This allowed the tree to be outside for everyone to enjoy both day and night. In addition, once the manufacturer found out that children would be participating, they'd donated additional cases.

"I know what I wish for." Clive, Betty's longtime beau and now husband after a simple spring wedding, entered the kitchen, his wish apparent by the sniffing gesture he was making. Indeed, the kitchen smelled of freshly baked chocolate chip cookies, and Mist fetched one, placed it on a china plate, and set it on the counter in front of him. She followed it with a mug of coffee. Clive rubbed his hands together and wasted no time testing both.

The holiday season was always special in the town of Timberton, Montana, and Christmas at the Timberton Hotel was the most special of all. From Mist's traditional Christmas Eve dinner to Betty's annual cookie exchange to the joy of new and returning guests sharing camaraderie in the hotel's front parlor, it was everyone's favorite time of year.

"And what will you wish for?" Betty directed this question to Mist. "Or do you believe wishes should be kept secret?"

"I think a person can choose to share or not share a wish." Mist took another sip of peppermint tea. "I don't think letting people know what you wish for keeps it from coming true."

"But what if it does?"

"Then perhaps it isn't really what you're wishing for."

"I'd better test that theory out." Clive jumped up and

approached the oven. He reached out with both hands and closed his eyes with dramatic flair. "I wish I'd find an apple pie baking in this oven." He opened the door with a mock harrumph. "You see? I shared what my wish was, and it didn't come true."

Mist stood and smiled. She moved to a ceramic jar on the counter and reached inside, pulling out a freshly baked treat and offering it to Clive. "Perhaps it's because your wish was really for a cinnamon scone."

"Ah, you may have a point there." Clive accepted the scone and immediately took a bite. "You're right! This must have been my wish. It's delicious."

Betty chuckled. "Just as delicious as the two you had this morning?"

"Absolutely. And now I have enough energy to go get some work done at the gallery." Clive finished off the scone and headed out.

"More like a sugar rush. That's what he has now!" Betty chuckled and then nodded toward the reservation book. "So who do we have coming this year? New guests, I mean. I know our regulars wouldn't miss Christmas at the Timberton Hotel."

Mist smiled. "They'll all be here: Clara and Andrew, Nigel, better known as the professor, and Michael, of course."

"I can't wait to hear where Clara and Andrew went this year," Betty said. "I love hearing about their annual trips."

"We get to travel with them when they tell us about their adventures," Mist mused. "Armchair travel." She opened the registration book and scanned the arrival list.

"And didn't the professor say that he had a surprise for us?" Betty tapped her fingers on the kitchen counter.

Mist looked up and smiled. "He did. And I think Michael knows what it is, but I can't even get a hint from him."

"That rascal," Betty said. "But you can't blame him if the professor told him in confidence."

"True," Mist agreed. "Michael would always honor a confidence. We'll just have to be patient and let the secret be revealed in its own time." She looked down at the registration book, noting a question mark she had placed by a vacant room. Michael had casually asked if the hotel kept an extra room ready, which was indeed something they did. It was always possible someone's car might break down while visiting the town or who needed a place to be with others for the holiday. She was eager to see what was behind the professor's mystery.

Betty leaned forward in an attempt to read the guest list herself but relaxed as Mist began to read.

"We have the Taylors, a couple from Washington. Spokane, if I recall. They're driving down."

Betty's eyebrows lifted. "Driving? Well, I guess it's not all that far. About four hours or so."

Mist nodded. "That's what Mrs. Taylor said when she made the reservation. They're planning to continue traveling after this and wanted the freedom of having their own car." She looked back down at the registration book. "We'll also have the Cooper family with us: two parents and two children. They're flying in from Tennessee."

"Boys or girls?" Betty asked, quickly following it with, "Oh, it doesn't matter! It will be lovely to have children here this year!"

Mist checked her notes. "One of each. Young but not toddlers, elementary school age, I think."

"How delightful!" Betty exclaimed. "It would be nice if the boy's about Clay Jr.'s age."

"True," Mist said. "I think Clay Jr. is five now."

"Exactly right." A new voice joined in as Maisie stepped into the kitchen, arms laden with flowers and greenery. "But he'd be sure to point out that he's five *and a half* if he heard this discussion."

Betty chuckled. "I'm sure he would."

"Lovely flowers, Maisie!" Mist stood and greeted her friend at the door, taking some of the foliage. She buried her face in the fresh blooms, eucalyptus, and pine cuttings. She closed her eyes and took a deep breath. The mixed scents took her to another world, a winter forest of fresh air, sweet scents, and magic.

"It looks like you girls have a project ahead of you." Betty took her coffee cup to the sink. "I have errands to run, so I'll leave you to it." Slipping on a jacket from a hook by the kitchen's side door, she grabbed a hat and gloves and left as Mist and Maisie moved into the café to decorate.

Chapter Two

Filtered sunlight flowed through the front windows of the café, weaving through tree branches in the hotel's front yard and casting an ethereal glow into the room. Maisie pushed two tables together while Mist set the mood with Christmas music by Pentatonix. Taking seats together at the newly formed worktable, they spread the makings for the centerpieces out before them, including small rustic pails that Mist had chosen to hold this year's arrangement.

"I see Clay Jr.'s not with you today." Mist lifted an ivory rose and twisted the stem back and forth.

Maisie laughed. "Are you kidding me? Clayton's parents just got into town last night. They're going to want as much grandparent time as possible with him."

"Which will give you some well-deserved time to yourself," Mist pointed out.

"Yes! And I plan to enjoy every minute of it."

Mist leaned forward and lowered her voice. "Have you told them yet?"

"Told them?" Maisie feigned confusion. "What would I possibly have to tell them?"

"Oh, I don't know...," Mist said, placing red cyclamen next to the rose, admiring the combination. "Maybe something about the fact your family is growing? That there will be a new addition next June?"

Maisie raised one finger in the air to signify a light-bulb moment. "Oh *that!* We're going to tell them on Christmas Eve."

"And Clay Jr.?"

"Also on Christmas Eve," Maisie said. "But a few hours earlier so he can feel he's getting the news first. Not any sooner because I doubt he could keep the secret."

"And Clayton?" Mist teased her, knowing full well that Maisie's husband would already know.

"Very funny."

"I'm excited for you, Maisie. It will be wonderful for Clay Jr. to have a brother or sister."

Maisie laughed. "He'll be hoping for a brother, I'm sure. He has a friend in his playgroup who has a baby brother, and he's been asking why he doesn't have one too."

"How are you feeling?" Mist knew Maisie was planning to help with the traditional Christmas Eve dinner at the Moonglow Café. "Please don't feel you have to help on Christmas Eve if it'll tire you. We can manage."

Maisie grabbed some greenery and began snipping the stems. "Don't worry about that. If anything, I have more energy than usual. No idea why. It wasn't like that with Clay Jr."

"I've heard each child can be different."

Maisie nodded. "True. For example, I was only hungry for certain foods with Clay Jr. This time, I swear I can eat anything I get my hands on. Speaking of which, what's on the menu for this year's feast?"

"A lovely selection, I think. Something for everyone. It's

one advantage of having a buffet, being able to serve a variety of choices." Mist had always favored a buffet over a plated meal. It could be just as elegant and yet give those dining more freedom. If something went against their own beliefs or simply didn't appeal to them, they could move on to another dish. No need to turn anything down verbally or leave something on their plate to be wasted.

"Such as?" Maisie nudged Mist to spill the menu.

"Brisket with fennel and rosemary as a main dish," Mist said, "which should please the carnivores. And a honey-thyme butternut squash quinoa casserole for others, as well as cranberry gnocchi with butter sauce."

Maisie sighed. "I wouldn't mind trying each of those right now. I don't suppose you have a test plate I could have in, say, five minutes?"

"I'm afraid you'll have to wait." Mist laughed. "Besides, you'll want the herb-roasted brussels sprouts and glazed Marsala carrots with hazelnuts to go with that. Which reminds me to have two serving dishes of those carrots, one without hazelnuts, in case there are guests with nut allergies."

"And dessert?"

"Spiced pear soufflé," Mist said. "Something a little different this time. Glenda had an old family recipe for it that looked wonderful. I tried it out on Michael, and he gave it a thumbs-up."

Maisie stood up and stretched, her hands rubbing her lower back. "Well, sign me up for a double serving of everything." She looked at a centerpiece that Mist had just finished. "Those will be wonderful. I'm glad we got the paperwhites to mix in."

"Yes. A perfect combination: roses, cyclamen, paperwhites, and assorted greenery. I have wire-edged red ribbon to tie around the pail handles too."

"Elegant, colorful, and rustic, all at the same time." Maisie nodded her approval and excused herself to go check on her household.

Alone again, Mist made quick but enjoyable work of finishing the centerpieces, pulling them together one by one and adding the bows at the end. Satisfied the table decorations were ready, she cleaned up the residual cuttings and ribbon scraps and moved on to her next task.

Mist stood before the hallway closet, her hand slipping around the cool metal doorknob. She always felt a shiver of excitement when she approached the small closet in the back hallway. It was a special place to her, a place to keep hidden treasure, much like a spot behind a loose brick where a message might be hidden in a forest wall, safely tucked away to be found later. Everyone knew it was her private realm. Even Betty and Michael knew better than to place items inside even if they found something they knew she might like to add to her stash. She would occasionally find something left outside the door, an offering for her collection, something someone else had found and thought she would like. She would then be the one to take the item inside, to find a home for it in a basket or box or metal tub.

It had been a good year for collecting treasures. She and Michael had traveled at times during the past year after their Christmas Eve wedding. Though she loved the usual Montana haunts she'd frequented for years—antique shops, thrift stores, anywhere she might find something whimsical or inspiring— she'd been delighted to explore new areas. Inspired by beaded crafts in Taos and Santa Fe, she'd gathered loose beads, leather strands, and jewelry findings to create the makings of an activity that future guests might enjoy. A trip along the Northern California coast had led her to gather bits and pieces of nature with varying textures: rocks, shells, feathers, driftwood. These she'd saved in a wooden bowl carved by a roadside artist in a seaside town.

These items and many others would provide finishing touches to guest rooms, unique bits of decor intended to inspire creativity or a sense of adventure. Nothing of tremendous monetary value went into the rooms, and nothing had ever been taken. But Mist believed that if something happened to go home with a guest, that item was meant to belong to them anyway. Perhaps the item itself might whisper "take me home" to a visitor, a silent request to become a part of that visitor's life.

Gathering her choices, she closed the closet door and visited each guest room upstairs, adding something unique to the soft winter throw blankets and holiday treats that had already been placed in each accommodation. She then returned downstairs and sorted through a stack of books she'd gathered at thrift stores, selecting several titles to add to the Little Free Library that the hotel had set up in the front yard, close to the sidewalk. In keeping with the season, she added a cookbook of holiday recipes, a delightful children's book about a snowman, several current novels, and two copies of Charles Dickens's *A Christmas Carol*, which both Michael and the professor had insisted were essential.

Finally, with the flowers arranged, the special touches to the guest rooms added, the Little Free Library restocked, beverage and sweets set up in the lobby, and most important of all, an open heart, the Timberton Hotel was ready for the holiday visitors.

Chapter Three

Mist heard the front door open and close, followed by the tapping of footsteps on the lobby floor. She emerged from the kitchen to find the first guests of the holiday weekend, Justine and Randall Taylor. The senior couple sported knit hats and gloves in festive holiday colors. Justine's red set boasted snowmen around a folded cuff on the hat. A matching snowman adorned the back of each glove. Randall's bright green hat had a similar pattern on the cuff but with candy canes instead of snowmen. Randall stood a good half foot taller than Justine, and both guests had rosy cheeks from the cold temperature outside.

"Welcome to the Timberton Hotel."

"Thank you," Justine said. "We're so excited to be here! Friends of ours stayed here a few years ago, and we've been wanting to visit ever since they told us about it." She looked around, her eyes beaming. "It's just as lovely as they said. And so full of holiday spirit!"

Mist followed the direction of the woman's gaze and smiled. It was true. The stairway leading up to the second floor looked enchanting with white lights twinkling from an ever-green garland along the banister. A poinsettia graced the registration counter, and elegant candles rose from small wreathes of holly on the beverage table. A cluster of mistletoe and red ribbon hung above the archway to the front parlor. Beyond that, a magnificent Christmas tree stood near the hotel's front picture window. Clive and Betty had insisted on doing the decorating for the holidays, and they'd done a magnificent job. A glance in any direction boasted a touch of Christmas cheer.

"And we're excited to have you," Mist said. "How was your trip here? Not too difficult, I hope."

"A few weather challenges," Randall said. "But that's to be expected with travel at this time of year."

"But we're here now," Justine said.

"And that's what counts," Mist replied. "Let's get you settled in your room, and then you can relax, whether resting upstairs or enjoying the front parlor. You may help yourself to beverages and treats anytime. Make sure you try Betty's glazed cinnamon nuts. And we'll have a fire going in the fireplace in just a bit."

"It sounds lovely!" Justine looked around again while Randall filled out a registration card.

Mist handed them a key. "Allow me to show you to your room." She gestured to the staircase, and Justine and Randall followed her up the stairs to a room several doors down one of two hallways.

"This is one of my favorite rooms," Mist said as she opened the door for them. A four-poster bed boasted a thick ivory quilt with matching pillow shams and a throw pillow with a forest print. A low table lay in front of plush, floral upholstered chairs with thick cushions, offering a comfortable sitting area. Decorative holiday touches graced the room in various places. A small vase with an ivory rose, green eucalyptus, and red berries rested on an antique dresser. A silver tray of candy canes and chocolates sat on the low table. And a small Christmas tree stood on a corner table, its branches adorned with clusters of baby's breath and red bows.

"Oh!" Justine brought one hand to her chest. "It's beautiful. It's like stepping into a dream."

"I'm glad you like it," Mist said. "I'll be downstairs if you need anything. Betty, the hotelkeeper, will also be available. Make yourselves at home. This is now your Christmas home."

With that, Mist returned downstairs. Within minutes, the front door opened again and a family of four entered.

"Welcome to the Timberton Hotel," Mist said, taking note of the two adults accompanied by two children—a girl of around eight years and a younger brother by two years or so. The children appeared uncertain about their Timberton vacation, but the parents were clearly excited.

"What a lovely hotel!" the woman exclaimed as she looked around the lobby. "We're the Coopers," she added by way of introduction. She glanced at her husband as if to verify this information, which Mist found somehow endearing.

"We're delighted to have you here, Mr. and Mrs. Cooper," Mist said before addressing the children directly. "And both of you too. This is a fun place to spend Christmas."

The older girl returned Mist's greeting with a smile. Her younger brother remained quiet but glanced around the room, somewhat shy but curious. Mist took this to be a good sign. It wouldn't take long for the children to feel at home. She felt certain both would settle in quickly. The hotel tended to have that effect on guests, regardless of their age or initial disposition.

"Please call us Lauren and Keith," the woman said. "And these are our children, Camille and Bennett."

"Ben," a soft voice whispered.

"Yes, I meant Ben." The woman winked. "I forget sometimes."

"I'll bring our bags in," Keith said.

"Would you like help?" Mist offered. "Clive is around somewhere. He can help with your luggage."

"I certainly can," Clive said, entering the lobby with an armful of firewood. "Just let me set this down." He dropped the wood off beside the front parlor's fireplace and stepped back into the lobby.

"Thank you," Keith said. "We only have a few bags, one for each of us. I'll take a couple of them. Our car is right out front." He and Clive stepped out to fetch the bags.

"I can't wait to explore this town," Lauren said as she filled out a registration card. "It's absolutely charming with all the little shops and festive decorations."

"There's so much to enjoy here." Mist lowered her voice to a whisper. "Even a new store with a soda fountain."

Clive and Keith returned quickly, and Mist showed them to their rooms, a second-floor suite that would let the children have their own room.

"Oh, this is wonderful," Lauren said as she took in the cheerful accommodations. The spacious layout of the rooms and common area resembled a winter wonderland. Mist and Betty had updated the decor in all the guest rooms for the holidays, adding quilts in holiday colors and throw pillows with whimsical stencils of snowflakes, snowmen, and nutcrackers. A sleigh-shaped container offering old-fashioned Christmas candy sat next to an arrangement of red carnations, holly, and miniature white chrysanthemums. A shimmering red-and-gold bow dressed up a clear jar filled with star-shaped sugar cookies.

"We get our own room?" Camille asked, her eyes wide.

Mist looked to the parents, though that had been her plan all along.

"Yes," Lauren said. "Isn't that great?" Both Camille and Ben nodded.

"I'll let you settle in," Mist said. "Feel free to enjoy the front parlor. We'll have a fire going shortly."

"Indeed we will," Clive said, setting down their luggage and excusing himself to finish stocking firewood.

"There's a bookshelf filled with reading material for all ages, a craft table, and a piano. We often have music playing too, especially Christmas music this time of year."

"Oh, I love music!" Camille exclaimed.

Lauren nodded. "She plays a little piano. Just picked it up by ear."

"That's wonderful, Camille! Feel free to play the one we have. There's also coffee, tea, and apple cider in the lobby. Help yourselves." Mist lowered her voice and leaned toward the children as if passing along a secret. "And hot chocolate."

"With marshmallows?" Ben asked.

"Of course!" Mist replied. "And peppermint sticks too."

Ben clapped his hands, and Camille looked pleased.

Assured that the Cooper family was set for their stay, Mist returned downstairs to await more arrivals.

Chapter Four

Clive had just built a welcoming fire in the front parlor when Clara and Andrew, longtime regulars for Christmas holiday visits, walked in the door. Andrew set two suitcases down by the registration desk and shook hands with Clive, who was the first to greet them.

Clara pulled off her gloves and hat, looking around. "It feels like we never left!" She accepted a hug from Clive.

"That's because you're home," Mist said. Having heard the front door, she'd come from the kitchen, passing through the café on the way.

"Our Christmas home," Clara said. "Yes, that's exactly what it feels like. I can't imagine spending the holidays anywhere else."

Betty was right behind Mist. More hugs were exchanged, and in short order, a registration card was completed. Clara and Andrew ascended the stairs to drop their luggage off in their guest room and soon returned downstairs. Clara settled into the front parlor to relax in front of the fire while Andrew fetched coffee from the beverage bar in the lobby. At Mist's gentle insistence, Betty and Clive sat down to visit.

Andrew returned with two mugs of Mist's Java Love. He handed one mug to Clara and took a seat beside her on the sofa. "I believe congratulations are in order," he said, grinning at Betty and Clive.

"Yes," Clive said, wrapping his arm around Betty's shoulders and pulling her close. "Poor thing. She's stuck with me now."

"Only if he behaves," Betty said, teasing. "And yes, we took the simple route, just like the two of you did. Quiet wedding at the courthouse, no crazy fanfare. Mist and Michael were our witnesses."

"We've been busy ever since. We expanded Betty's room here in the back of the hotel," Clive said. "Amazing what a difference a few feet can make in a small space. We only gained about four feet in all that work. It doesn't sound like much, but the room feels like it's twice the size."

"Well, consider the building," Betty said. "Old hotels typically had small rooms. Many still do, and this one is no exception. Guest quarters weren't as extravagant as they are these days in newer hotels."

"Our room is pretty big," Andrew noted. "And very comfortable. There's plenty of space to move around."

"That's because that room was remodeled years ago," Betty said. "Decades ago, actually. The entire upstairs was remodeled back in the seventies to accommodate modern travelers. But the downstairs rooms remained the same."

Mist smiled as she excused herself to quickly check on the kitchen, thinking of the room she'd used for years before moving into the old café building with Michael. She still used it for a studio and occasional overnight stays when the hotel was full. The coziness of the room was part of its charm.

"Catch us up on other Timberton happenings," Clara said. She reached for a crystal dish on a side table and took a glazed cinnamon nut, popping it into her mouth. She closed her eyes, sighed, and immediately helped herself to another. "Mmm. I look forward to these every year!"

"It's been a busy year," Clive said. "I expanded the gallery, for one thing."

"Really?" Clara exclaimed. "What a wonderful idea! Is this to give more room to art?"

"Exactly," Clive said. "And not just paintings. We have local artists who work with different mediums. Textile art, for example. And glasswork by a guy who moved into the area last spring."

Clara beamed. "I can't wait to see! What a wonderful idea, opening the gallery to local artists."

"Visitors to town love it," Betty said. "It gives them an option to take home something special to remember their visit by."

"We hope to offer classes in the spring," Clive added, "and Mist is developing plans for some children's workshops."

"Those are made by a local potter." Betty nodded toward the mugs Clara and Andrew were holding.

Clara and Andrew both looked at their coffee mugs, noting the forest-green glaze and pine tree design.

"I knew we hadn't seen these before," Clara said. "They're lovely. I hope we can buy a pair to take home. I'm guessing they're in the new gallery area?"

"Indeed they are. Speaking of which..." Clive stood up and clapped his hands. "I'd better get back and make sure things are under control. I left Michael there to handle the place while I came over to build the fire. Extra firewood is over there." He pointed to a metal container with wood next to the fireplace.

"I can keep it going," Andrew offered.

"You're a good man, Andrew," Clive called over his shoulder as he headed for the front door.

Betty also stood, ready to excuse herself to help Mist in the kitchen. "There's another new place you'll have to check out: Duffy's. It was quite a mystery at first but a delightful surprise for the town."

"Duffy's?" Clara repeated, curious. "Is it a shop? A restaurant? A bakery? Something else?"

"I hope not a restaurant," Andrew said. "I'd hate to see something compete with the Moonglow Café."

"Nothing could ever compete with the Moonglow Café," Clara pointed out.

Andrew nodded. "You have a point there."

"You'll just have to see it for yourselves," Betty said. "You can be as surprised as the rest of us were when it opened."

"An excursion is in order then!" Clara took a sip of her coffee and then held the mug up to admire it. At the sound of the front door, she turned that way, as did everyone else. All were delighted to see Nigel Hennessy step into the lobby. To everyone's surprise, a young lady accompanied him.

"Professor!" Betty exclaimed. "So good to see you! And I know who this is..." She tapped a finger against her lips, her memory searching for the name.

"Poppy!" Clara grinned, recognizing the professor's niece from a previous Christmas visit years ago.

Mist pulled Poppy into a soft embrace. "We're so excited to see you," she said as she stepped back.

"I'm excited to be here," Poppy said, her London accent enchanting everyone in the room.

"So this is your surprise," Betty said, eyeing the professor. "And a delightful surprise it is!"

The professor looked at his niece with obvious pride. "Poppy will be here as an exchange student this coming semester. She'll be staying in student housing at the university."

Betty turned to Mist and smiled. "Michael did a good job keeping this a secret."

Mist gave Poppy a mischievous smile. "He certainly did."

"Care for some hot tea, Professor?" Mist offered. "PG Tips, your favorite."

"That would be brilliant," the professor replied. "I think I'll dash upstairs to put our things away and then return down here to enjoy tea by the fire."

"I'll get your keys." Mist stepped back into the lobby and returned with two keys. "You have your regular accommodation, Professor, and the other key is for the extra room. I'm delighted to now know who will be staying in it." She turned to Poppy and smiled. "I think you'll find it lovely."

"I'm sure it will be. I may have been younger when I was here before, but I remember clearly that *everything* was lovely." Poppy glanced around the front parlor. "Absolutely a world of its own. Is that candy store still here? I remember that and also the sapphire and art gallery."

Mist smiled, always enchanted to know what memories lingered after a visit to Timberton. Memories were the one thing she knew guests would take with them, and it was her goal to create the best ones possible.

"Yes," Betty answered. "Marge still has her candy shop. And Clive runs the gallery you're remembering. You'll have to visit both."

"Indeed I will." Poppy beamed with excitement.

"Have others arrived?" The professor took the two keys from Mist and handed Poppy hers.

"Yes," Mist said. "A lovely family of four from Tennessee and a couple from Washington State. You'll meet them at dinner."

"Splendid!" The professor turned to Poppy. "Ready to get settled in?"

"Absolutely." Poppy beamed. "I'm ready for everything about this adventure! I've wished for it for a long time."

"We'll be back down to visit in a bit," the professor said. "At least I will. I suspect the younger of us will head off in search of sweets."

Betty chuckled. "Marge will be delighted to see you, Poppy."

Mist watched as the professor and Poppy headed upstairs, then turned back to the front parlor. The soothing warmth of the fire, the sparkling lights on the Christmas tree, and other seasonal touches around the hotel blended together to create a magical holiday atmosphere. And now the most important part of it all had been added: the guests.

Chapter Five

THE SOUND OF THE FRONT DOOR OPENING AND CLOSING preceded footsteps in the lobby. A shuffling indicative of coats being removed and hung up followed, after which Clara stepped into the parlor, Andrew just behind.

Clara took a seat by the fireplace and wrapped her arms around her shoulders. "We thought a late afternoon stroll would be a good idea, but it's a little chilly out there!"

"That's winter in Montana," Betty said, turning from the Christmas tree where she'd been admiring a new handmade ornament dropped off by a local child. "There's hot mulled cider in the lobby. That should warm you up before dinner, which is only an hour from now."

Andrew did an immediate about-face. "Two mugs coming up!" He returned quickly, handing one mug to Clara and holding the other up to the room. "Anyone else?" Noting others already had their own, he took a seat near Clara.

"So tell us about your travels this past year," the professor said. "You always take a midyear trip. Where did you go this time?"

"Egypt!" Clara exclaimed. "Can you believe it? Andrew suggested it. He's always wanted to see the pyramids."

"Yes," Andrew said. "I've dreamed of seeing them since I was a boy. I became fascinated with them when we studied them in school. My curiosity only grew over the years."

Clara cupped a hand around her mouth and whispered, "Many years."

Andrew rolled his eyes and laughed. "Only a few decades," he countered.

"Six," Clara whispered again before turning to her husband. "Or is it seven? You did just have a birthday."

Andrew patted Clara's knee and cleared his throat. "Yes, dear. You may have a point there."

"It must have been amazing to see the pyramids up close," Randall said. "We've talked about visiting Egypt one day, haven't we?" He glanced at Justine, who nodded.

"It was," Andrew said. "Truly mind-boggling.

Clara nodded. "We had a fabulous view of the largest pyramid from our hotel. And a wonderful guide gave us a tour once we got there."

"Are they tall?" Ben asked.

"Very tall," Clara said. "Especially the biggest one."

The professor piped up. "That would be the one built by Khufu. It was approximately 481 feet in height when it was built. But erosion over the years has brought it down to about 456 feet."

"Taller than this, right?" Ben jumped up, raised both hands over his head, and wobbled on tiptoes.

"Much taller than that," the professor said, smiling.

"Could you go inside?" Poppy asked.

"Yes, but not everywhere," Andrew said. "We were able to go into some sections, but others were off-limits."

Clara nodded. "It was fascinating going inside, although I found it a little claustrophobic."

"That didn't bother me," Andrew said, "but it would have helped to be shorter. Those inner corridors were not built for six-foot-tall visitors."

"Did you see hieroglyphics?" Camille asked. "We studied about them in school this year."

"There aren't any in the three Giza pyramids, though there are some in other pyramids," Andrew said. "We only saw some at the base of the Sphinx."

"Oh! You saw that too?" Ben said. "The giant cat statue?"

Clara was not the only one to smile. "It does look a little like a cat, doesn't it? But it's actually an animal body with a human head on top."

Ben wrinkled his forehead. "Weird."

"Quite weird," the professor said, sounding chipper.

Justine tilted her head. "I've heard the Sphinx's nose is gone because of Napoleon's army using it for target practice. Is that true?"

Andrew shook his head. "We thought that too. But it turns out that's probably a myth. The Sphinx lost its nose before Napoleon even visited Egypt."

The professor spoke up. "The prominent theory is that it was destroyed in the fifteenth century by a man named Muhammad Sa'im al-Dahl. Sketches by Frederic Louis Norden, a Danish naval officer and cartographer, were published in 1755. They show the Sphinx's nose already damaged. Napoleon did not enter Egypt until 1798."

"As always, Professor," Clara said, "you are a fountain of information."

"What's a cartographer?" Ben asked.

Keith ruffled his son's hair. "A person who makes maps."

Mist, having enjoyed the tail end of the conversation while

approaching from the café, spoke up. "Perhaps some of you might like a map to a soup-and-salad bar?"

Andrew stood up without hesitation, and the others followed, all heading toward the café.

"What a great meal for dinner on a cold night!" Clara exclaimed. "I do love hot soup in the winter."

Mist greeted locals who entered the hotel as the guests passed through the lobby on the way from the front parlor to the café. Sally accompanied William Guthrie, as most had come to expect now. Millie, Marge, and Glenda arrived together, planning to use the dinner hour to go over notes for the library's movie event the following night. And Clayton's parents stopped in to enjoy the café camaraderie and to allow Maisie, Clayton, and Clay Jr. a quiet dinner hour at home.

The varied buffet selections allowed everyone to find something appealing. Each of three tureens offered butternut squash soup, potato soup, or a hearty minestrone. Salad choices included a mixed green salad with optional toppings, a spinach salad with strawberries, and a Moroccan carrot salad with golden raisins and peanuts. A basket at the end of the buffet held sourdough rolls, and a tray offered an assortment of cookies, heavy on the chocolate chip side.

"I also have mac and cheese hidden in the kitchen," Mist whispered to Ben and Camille. Ben's eyes lit up, and Camille smiled. Lauren whispered a thank-you, adding that two servings, one for each child, would be wonderful.

"Make that three," Poppy said, overhearing the inside scoop as she entered. "I love macaroni cheese."

"It's *mac and* cheese," Ben said, giving Poppy a funny look.

"Ah, right you are! But we usually call it macaroni cheese in the UK." Poppy scooted into a seat beside Ben. "Sometimes the same thing is called something different in different places," she explained.

Ben let out a big sigh. "Weird."

"His favorite word lately," Lauren whispered to Poppy.

Tables and chairs filled quickly, and Nat King Cole's smooth voice soon floated through the café, telling of chestnuts roasting on an open fire.

"Did you know that's not the name of that song?" The professor, who'd taken a seat at a table with Justine and Randall, piped up. He directed his question to no one in particular, but several responded.

"Chestnuts roasting on an open fire?" Andrew's eyebrows lifted.

"Correct," the professor said. "Meaning *not* correct."

Justine tilted her head. "We always called it that growing up, but now that I think about it..." She turned to her husband.

"It's technically called 'The Christmas Song,'" Randall said.

"Correct again," the professor said. "Written in 1944 by Mel Tormé and Bob Wells."

"You should really go on a trivia show, Uncle Nigel," Poppy said, to which he just tutted.

"Well, I can see how that song title could be confusing," Justine said. "There are so many Christmas songs. If someone asked me to play 'The Christmas Song,' I'd be likely to ask which one."

A new song followed, this time Perry Como telling the tale of a little drummer boy. As a selection of Christmas songs continued, guests and local diners helped themselves to soups—some trying all three—and salads, finally turning to the brownies, some of which were carried into the front parlor to be enjoyed in front of the fire.

"Ready for a bit of chess despair?" the professor asked Andrew, his expression one of both challenge and humor.

Andrew rubbed his hands together eagerly. "I've waited all

year for this." He accompanied the professor to a small table to the side of the fireplace where a chess set stood waiting.

"I'll watch," Keith said as Lauren settled at a craft table with Ben and Camille. "I've always been curious about the game."

"It hails back 1,500 years to the game of *chaturanga* in India...," the professor began as he sat down and indicated a nearby seat for Keith.

"He's incorrigible," Poppy said as she patted her uncle's shoulder affectionately. "Once I get settled at the university, I'm going to call him when I need to research anything instead of going to the library."

"I don't think so, dear Poppy," the professor quipped.

Poppy grinned as she ran an index finger along a row of books, debating her reading options. Choosing a collection of short stories, she settled into a comfortable chair near the Christmas tree.

"Your travel to Egypt sounded wonderful earlier, Clara," Lauren said. "How we'd love to take a trip like that if we can ever get the time."

Keith nodded. "Even something closer. We've talked about taking a riverboat up the Mississippi. It's just a matter of finding a chance to get away."

"It's not easy when you're raising a family," Justine said. "Randall and I know that well. We raised three children and juggled busy careers through it all: hospital administration for me and corporate law for Randall. It was impossible to get away."

"What about now?" Clara asked.

"Now, honestly? We just retired recently, and the kids are all grown with their own families. All we want to do now is relax." Justine gestured to the bookcases. "I would love a long stretch of reading time—I'm talking *months,* uninterrupted—to just read."

"I feel the same way," Randall said. "Reading has always been a passion of mine. I need to catch up on anything that's not a law brief."

Together, once dinner cleanup was complete, Mist and Betty stood side by side under the archway, watching the guests relaxing. Clive stopped by to restock the firewood, pausing to point up at the mistletoe above Betty's head before giving her a quick kiss. And Mist, once assured that everyone was comfortable and settled in for the evening, excused herself and retired to her art room. Although the guests had barely arrived, she already had ideas for the souvenirs she always sent home with them at the end of their stay. It was time to get started.

Chapter Six

An early morning hint of dawn and light snowfall welcomed Mist as she set up the coffee and tea in the lobby so it would be ready for guests. She'd planned a baked strata with tomatoes, mushrooms, and spinach for breakfast, an easy casserole to bake and serve. Bacon would be offered on the side as well as home fries and a bowl of fresh melon.

"Good morning," Betty said cheerfully, entering the kitchen just as Mist popped the strata in the oven. "What can I do to help?"

Mist smiled. "How about having a cup of coffee and sitting to visit?"

"I think I can manage that." Betty chuckled as she poured herself a mug of coffee from the kitchen's coffee pot, which was always going, separate from the service in the front lobby. She took a seat at the kitchen island and was soon joined by Clive, who grabbed another coffee.

"Just what I need," Clive announced. He blew across the coffee mug to help cool the steaming beverage.

"You'll have a busy day with Christmas shoppers, I'm sure," Betty said.

Clive nodded. "I'm counting on it. I'm glad I have help."

"I think Michael will be there today," Mist said.

"Yes." Clive took a cautious sip of coffee. "He's working part of the day, and I have a couple of high school kids helping later."

Mist slid a cheesy egg casserole into the oven and set pans on two burners, one for potatoes that were already cut and ready to fry. The other would serve for bacon, which she soon had sizzling. The aromas of breakfast fare soon wafted from the kitchen, beckoning guests from their rooms. They could enjoy having coffee, tea, and miniature blueberry muffins in the front parlor until the café opened.

"The gallery is busier since opening that second area," Betty said. "Expanding was a wonderful idea."

"Especially since it allows other local artists to exhibit their work." Mist moved a batch of bacon onto paper towels and placed more in the pan.

Betty started to speak again when a tapping sound began to rattle through the kitchen. Clive, the first to recognize the sound, grabbed a piece of bacon, tore off a piece, and innocently dropped it on the floor. Betty playfully batted his arm in reprimand.

"Bacon, is that you?" Mist said, grinning. "You know you're not allowed in the kitchen." The only response she received, as expected, was the smacking sound of a sweet dog enjoying the sneaky treat from Clive.

The back door between the kitchen and hallway quickly opened, and Hollister, the town's formerly homeless person who now lived downstairs in the hotel, stepped in. He looked at Mist and signed, "Sorry." Mist, having made a point of learning basic American Sign Language phrases during the past year, replied, "It's okay." She placed another piece of bacon on a paper towel and handed it to Hollister to take with him.

"Thank you," Hollister signed.

"You're welcome," Mist signed. After receiving a pat on the head, Bacon followed Hollister out of the kitchen.

"I just love that little dog," Betty said. "It was wonderful of Hollister to rescue him last year."

"He's the hotel's official greeter now," Clive pointed out. "Whenever he's upstairs, that is."

"I enjoy having him around," Mist agreed. "And Hollister's very good about keeping him downstairs when we have guests with allergies."

"Maybe I should think about getting a four-legged greeter for the gallery."

Mist nodded, pleased to hear the suggestion. "There are so many dogs who need homes. Cats too. Perhaps a gallery cat?"

"I like that idea!" Betty turned to Clive, beaming. "A gallery cat would be wonderful. Customers would love it."

Clive's eyebrows lifted as he considered the idea. "Not a bad suggestion. I'll think about it. Meanwhile..." He stood up and reached for his jacket. "I'd better get down there and help. I have customers picking up custom jewelry orders today. And I need to restock a few displays. I seem to be low on some items..." He cleared his throat with dramatic flair.

Mist laughed. "I can get more mini paintings to you tomorrow." She scooped home fries into a pottery serving bowl for the buffet and placed a generous serving in a reusable plastic container, which she handed to Clive.

"Excellent! The paintings *and* the taters!" Clive added a few strips of bacon to the potatoes and headed out.

"I wish he *would* get a gallery cat," Betty said after he left. "It's a wonderful idea. Customers would love it. I've seen bookstores that have resident cats. Why not a gallery?"

Mist carried the home fries and bacon out to the buffet and opened the café doors to eager breakfast customers. Betty followed with the cheesy egg casserole and a platter of assorted melon slices. Accompanied by upbeat holiday music, hotel guests and townsfolk alike mixed conversation with a morning meal that would start the day off on a cheerful note. With holiday tasks calling, most left soon after enjoying the meal.

"I'm going to head over to the library and help Millie set up for movie night," Betty said once the café and kitchen were cleaned up. She dried her hands on a kitchen towel and set it by the sink.

"She'll appreciate the help, I'm sure," Mist said. "How many people does she expect?"

Betty lifted a coat off a hook by the kitchen's back door and grabbed gloves and a knit cap from a nearby basket. "Hard to say since this is the first time the library has done this. But I know Marge has been making massive amounts of Christmas popcorn."

Mist laughed. "That alone should bring people in."

"Mmmm." Betty grinned. "With white chocolate and M&Ms added, you'd better believe it!"

MORNING EASED INTO THE AFTERNOON, and the light snowfall earlier turned into a crisp, sunny day. Mist was in the process of contemplating a variety of vegetables and herbs in a kitchen basket when she heard a soft tapping on the kitchen door. Setting the basket aside, she followed the sound and found Lauren on the other side, both children in tow.

"I thought I'd take the kids down to that soda fountain you told us about. It's at the new market?"

"Yes," Mist replied enthusiastically, happy to be sending

Duffy business. "In fact, if you don't mind, I'll accompany you. I was just realizing I may need fresh thyme."

Both Camille and Ben smiled and clapped their hands. "Yes! Come with us, Mist," Camille said.

"Perfect," Lauren said. "I was going to ask for directions, but a personal escort is much better." She turned to the kids. "Let's get your coats." Both children took off for the stairs to their room.

"Please don't run," Lauren called as she hurried after them.

Mist did a quick check in the kitchen to see what else she might need. She then grabbed a burgundy cape she kept in the front lobby and was soon met by Lauren, Camille, and Ben. Together, they left the hotel and started down the sidewalk.

"This is such a lovely town," Lauren said as she glanced around at the peaceful winter scene. "Almost like a fairy tale."

Mist was not surprised to hear this. She'd heard it before from other guests and often thought the same herself. There was indeed something almost magical about Timberton, something that couldn't be defined. Of course, Mist felt it had much to do with the combined energies of townsfolk as well as visitors. This made the already picturesque town even more charming than its mere physical character, which was both quaint and alluring. But there was something more, something undefinable yet very real.

"Yes," Mist said. "I agree."

"Hey, look," Ben said, pointing at a shop window. "It's a snowman, and it lights up." He pressed his face to the window. "And there's lots of candy!"

Mist smiled, pleased to see the display that Marge had set up in the window of her candy shop. The glowing snowman was surrounded by baskets of candy, everything from gumdrops to chocolate kisses to candy canes to Betty's favorites, caramels.

"Can we go in?" Camille asked, having caught her brother's enthusiasm.

Lauren looked at Mist. "Do you mind?"

"Of course not," Mist said. "Marge loves visitors, especially children! I'd like to say hello anyway."

Once inside the crowded shop, it became obvious that holiday shoppers needed all of Marge's attention. Even with two college-aged seasonal employees, it was hard to keep up with the demand. Still, Marge spotted them and waved them over to a side counter and offered the children a treat.

"Would you like to taste the Christmas popcorn?" Marge whispered. "It's a new, secret recipe."

"Yes!" Ben and Camille leaned forward as Marge held up a sample plate.

"Just a tiny bit," Lauren cautioned. "We're on our way to the soda fountain."

"Oh, Duffy's! You'll love it!" Marge nodded with enthusiastic approval and then hurried back to work.

Lauren herded the children to the front door, weaving through the crowd. Mist followed behind, accepting greetings from local townsfolk along the way. Once outside, they regrouped on the sidewalk.

"Ready for an old-fashioned soda now?" Mist asked, receiving affirmative nods from all. "All right. Let's go."

Chapter Seven

Timberton had always had a small market, one that provided the town with basic staples, though most residents, Mist included, made trips to the nearest larger town where they could find a full selection of provisions. This year had brought a change, one that eventually delighted the town and perhaps Mist most of all.

The elderly couple who had run the small store for many years had decided to retire in the spring. The townsfolk had been sorry to see them go but understood the decision. They bid farewell to the kindly seniors and began making longer drives to pick up groceries. A weekly farmer's market in Timberton during June, July, and August made the trips out of town less frequent than they would have been otherwise, but most residents still made them a couple of times per month. Mist made them more frequently, as she often needed specific ingredients for the meals she prepared for the Moonglow Café. In general, this is what everyone did for grocery shopping. It became the norm. That is, until Duffy O'Brien came to town.

Tall, thin, and terse of countenance, the Irishman—one

could only assume by his name—arrived unannounced the second week of September in a moving van, which he parked directly in front of the former market and a small adjacent building that had been empty for many years. The truck remained for several days, and when it departed, all that could be seen were two storefronts with windows covered with butcher paper. Attempts to see inside were futile. Much hammering and crashing from within indicated activity inside, but knocks on the front doors went unanswered.

It was as if a mystery had descended upon the town of Timberton. Townsfolk exchanged guesses among themselves as to what was going on behind the papered windows, but no one seemed to know. It was not unusual to see people gather across the street, hoping to glean information, even a small clue they could pass on to others.

"You don't suppose it's one of those fancy-type clothing stores, do you?" Clive had mused one day. He'd poured a cup of coffee from a thermos and passed it to Clayton. The two had taken a seat on a bench in the town's central park area.

"I doubt it," Clayton had replied. "Can't see that here in this town. What about a bookstore? Michael would love that."

"So would the professor. Though he and Michael both have access to plenty of books up at the university. And Millie does a great job keeping up the library offerings."

"Household goods?"

"Camping equipment?"

"A day spa?"

"Twenty bucks says it's a hardware store," Clive said.

"Twenty bucks says you're wrong." Clayton laughed.

Most everyone in the town ventured a guess at one point or another as to what was going on behind those papered windows. But it was to no avail. Even when a company arrived and placed a sign above the door, it did nothing more than identify the new business—that much they already knew, as it was a commercial location—as Duffy's. Nothing more.

Finally the day arrived without fanfare of any kind. It was just a day like any other day when the townsfolk discovered the windows cleared of butcher paper and the front doors propped open. News traveled quickly, as tends to happen in a small town, and soon the new business was filled with curious and delighted people. For a step into Duffy's was like a step into the past. The eccentric shopkeeper had managed to create the ambiance and appearance of an old-fashioned store while carrying everything townsfolk and visitors might need.

Pine display tables—built by Duffy himself—boasted a selection of fresh fruit that varied according to availability yet always included a variety of apples, one or two types of melons, and the usual assortment of pears, oranges, lemons, limes, and tomatoes. Baskets, tilted at convenient levels, held potatoes, onions, and garlic. A refrigerated section that Duffy had artistically enclosed in a rustic wooden structure offered berries and other produce that needed to remain chilled. To Mist's particular delight, Duffy managed to provide most of the fresh herbs that she used for cooking.

The rest of the grocery section followed the same pattern of decor. Staples such as flour, sugar, grains, and nuts were offered in bulk so customers could purchase what they needed by scooping the provisions from barrels. Canned goods stood in creative stacks on tables, and an enchanting section of sweets tempted shoppers with treats from Marge's candy store, just down the block. If customers inquired about items the store didn't carry, those items seemed to magically appear before their next shopping excursion.

To everyone's surprise and delight, the side wall of the formerly empty building—the wall dividing the two buildings having been knocked down during all the hammering and pounding—had been turned into a soda fountain, complete with a counter and four vinyl stools. A large painting of a root beer float graced the wall, and a selection of sweet syrups stood in a proud line along the back counter, old-fashioned soda glasses alongside.

Duffy himself was somewhat of an enigma. His appearance, a style that could most accurately be described as part hippie, part farmer, brought something new to the town in the form of the overalls-clad, salt-and-pepper ponytailed character. In spite of his keen ability to know what townsfolk wanted, he offered up little information about himself. When asked where he came from, he would simply say "the East Coast." If someone asked if he had family, he answered "a few." Mist had taken this on as a personal challenge, half out of curiosity and half out of a genuine desire to draw the man out and enfold him in the community. In time, Duffy had opened up a bit, and he and his store had become a part of the Timberton community.

Mist accompanied Lauren into the store and escorted them to the soda fountain. Duffy, seeing them come in, sauntered over to serve them.

"What'll it be for you fine folks today?" he said as they climbed onto stools at the counter. Ben's and Camille's eyes grew wide as Lauren read choices off the chalkboard menu on the wall. Cherry soda, chocolate egg cream, root beer float, vanilla malt. It all sounded good, and decisions didn't come easily.

"I think sodas for all," Lauren said, looking to Mist, who shook her head.

"Three then," Lauren said, turning to the children. "What flavor would you like? There's... Oh my..." She looked at the flavor options for sodas. "Chocolate, cherry, vanilla, orange, butterscotch, pineapple, huckleberry, and caramel."

"Wow, so many choices," Camille mused. "I'll have chocolate please."

"Cherry for me," Ben said. "How about you, Mom?"

"Hmm... butterscotch is tempting, but I'm going to go with huckleberry."

"Coming right up!" Duffy placed three old-fashioned soda glasses in front of a row of bottles with pumps. He squirted the specified syrup flavor in each glass and added seltzer to create a fizzy, flavorful drink for each order.

Lauren looked around and caught Mist's attention. "Nothing for you?"

"She has a standing order," Duffy said, placing a glass of iced green tea on the counter.

"Thank you, Duffy." Mist took a sip of the cool drink and turned toward the room, watching the activity while the others enjoyed their sodas. Several customers browsed a gift section of kitchen-related items. Glenda from the Curl 'n' Cue salon placed a bag of fresh cranberries in a shopping basket. Ernie from Pop's Parlor, the local watering hole, filled a grocery bag with limes while holding another already filled with lemons. Although new, Duffy's had become an integral part of the community already.

Mist turned back to the counter and smiled as she watched Ben and Camille enjoying their sodas. Duffy had excused himself to help again at the register.

"What do you want to be when you grow up?" Mist asked Ben.

"A fireman," Ben said without hesitation. "I want to wear that red hat they get to wear and drive a big fire truck."

"I believe he means it," Lauren said. "That answer never changes. He's said that since he was two years old."

Mist smiled, the beginning of an idea forming as she turned

to Camille. "And you?" Mist felt sure she knew what Camille's response would be but was in for a surprise.

"I want to be an astrophysicist." Camille delivered the answer firmly, as committed to it as her younger brother was to his aspiration.

"Really. Not a musician?"

Camille gave Mist a look of innocent confusion. "Of course, a musician too. There's music among the stars."

And with that, Mist knew she'd found a kindred spirit.

Chapter Eight

THE SUBTLE AROMAS OF GARLIC AND OREGANO GREETED guests as they entered the café. Peaceful jazz renditions of Christmas carols flowed from the sound system, and votive candles flickered on tabletops, adding even more atmosphere to the room that was already welcoming. Although the Christmas Eve dinner was always the highlight of the season, each evening meal offered an enchanting holiday ambiance. In truth, every meal at the Moonglow Café was special regardless of the time of year. But Christmas held its own sentimental charm.

Clayton, often the first to arrive—provided his fire chief duties didn't prevent it—showed up with his two visiting parents as well as Clay Jr. The family took seats at a large table that would allow Maisie a chance to sit with her husband, son, and in-laws should she get a break from helping Mist in the kitchen, something she often insisted on doing.

Lauren and Keith were the next to enter, accompanied by their children. Camille's eyes scanned the room with wonder as if she'd just stepped into a fairy tale setting. Ben took a more hesitant look around, but his spirits seemed to lift upon seeing

Clay Jr. and realizing there was someone in his age group there among all the adults.

Table by table, the café filled as guests and townsfolk arrived. The professor and Poppy took a table with Clara and Andrew. William Guthrie—known to all as Wild Bill but now regarded as not-so-wild in view of his fairly new relationship—showed up with Sally from Second Hand Sally's and took a table for two. Mist smiled as she watched him pull out a chair for Sally. Although the two had been seeing each other for a year now, it still seemed amazing to see Wild Bill, formerly gruff by most accounts, behaving like a gentleman. Even Wild Bill's, long regarded as a greasy spoon type of establishment, seemed to have improved. There was no doubt in anyone's mind that Sally had something to do with this. At her suggestion, the diner building had been divided in two, making the casual eaterie smaller—not a problem since rarely could more than two or three customers be found there—and adding a general store of sorts in the other half of the building. The building frontage, helped by a fresh coat of paint, looked quite catchy from the outside with one sign saying WILD BILL'S and the one right next to it identifying the store as ALSO BILL'S. The name had started as a joke but quickly became a favorite. Sally now spent half of her time manning the counter at the quirky store and the rest of her time at Second Hand Sally's.

Mist circled the room, greeting guests and filling water glasses. She nodded a hello to Justine and Randall as they entered and chose seats at a table with a few locals. As was typical for the last days before Christmas, the crowd was relatively small. Townsfolk often had family plans around the holidays, and some chose to wait for the traditional Christmas Eve meal to come to the café. Betty and Maisie emerged from the kitchen with oversized casserole dishes of lasagna, one with meat and one without. These they placed on the buffet alongside an antipasto salad and generous baskets of garlic bread.

Clive showed no bashfulness about being first to head for the buffet. He gestured to the Coopers, encouraging them to follow, which they did, plates in hand. As they reached the serving area, he stepped aside, allowing them to go ahead. Lauren and Keith helped their children fill their plates and then served themselves.

"We won't go hungry tonight!" Clive quipped, spying the Italian feast.

"When do we ever here?" Clayton laughed as he encouraged his parents to join in. One by one, others followed until the room filled with the cheerful sounds of silverware clinking on dishes and conversations being shared.

Mist circled the room, checking with guests to see if they needed anything. Once reassured that everyone was comfortable, she retreated to the kitchen, soon emerging with a large serving platter of double-chocolate-fudge brownies. She placed it at the end of the buffet, offering a convenient help-yourself dessert for those looking for something sweet to finish off the meal.

"Hey, Mist," Clive called out, seeing her setting the dessert tray down. "What time is that shindig over at the library tonight?"

"What shindig?" Andrew asked between bites of garlic bread.

The professor cleared his throat. "I believe the event Clive is referring to as a *shindig* is the Holiday Movie Night."

"Yes," Clara said. "I saw a flyer for it. They're showing *Miracle on 34th Street*, the original. I just love the part where they drop Santa's letters on the judge's desk! It's one of my favorite movies of all time."

"Mine too," Lauren said. "I watch it every year." She

turned to Keith. "We should go. What do you think? Bundle up and take the kids?"

"Sounds like a good plan to me."

"Will there be popcorn?" Poppy asked.

"I'm sure there will," Mist said, catching up with the enthusiastic conversation. "Not only regular popcorn but also a special Christmas mix that Marge let Ben and Camille try at the candy shop today."

"Splendid!" Poppy exclaimed. "I'd like to go." She turned to the professor. "What do you think, Uncle Nigel?" This brought smiles to quite a few in the room. No one was used to hearing the professor addressed by his actual name much less with "uncle" in front of it.

"I believe the chessboard is calling my name tonight," the professor said. "I promised Randall a match. But you should go."

"You have my sympathy, Randall," Andrew quipped, eliciting laughter from others. "I have yet to win a game against him."

"You can walk over to the library with us," Lauren offered, directing her comment to Poppy.

"Yeah!" Ben said. "We want Poppy to come with us."

"I'd love to." Poppy smiled at Ben.

Clay Jr., overhearing the conversation, turned to his dad. "Can I go too? I want Christmas popcorn."

"Andrew and I are going," Clara said to Clayton. "Clay Jr. can go with us. Or he might want to go with the other children." She looked at Lauren.

"Of course!" Lauren said. "The children can all go together. As well as the young lady." She and Poppy exchanged smiles. Now that she was a university student, Poppy could hardly be considered a child.

Clayton stood up, lifting his plate. "Well, now that that's

settled, I'm going for more lasagna." He headed for the buffet, Clive and William Guthrie right behind him.

As others helped themselves to seconds, Mist made the rounds of the room again, checking to see if anyone needed anything. Seeing that all was under control, she did a quick sweep of the kitchen—Betty and Clive had forbidden her to help with cleanup—the lobby, and the front parlor, and then settled into her small studio room to enjoy an hour to herself before heading to the library.

Chapter Nine

A buzz of excitement filled the air just outside the library. Voices flowed out onto the walkway as the doors opened and closed for people to enter. The event had proved a popular draw, confirming that Millie's decision to hold a movie night had been a great idea.

Michael held the door open for Mist, Lauren, Poppy, and the kids. Keith followed a few yards behind, having fallen into conversation with Andrew on the short walk over from the hotel. All mixed in with a stream of locals. Just about the whole town seemed to have turned out for the evening event, everyone enthusiastic. Well, almost everyone.

"I wouldn't have missed this for all the wishes on that glorious tree out there," Sally said, nudging William Guthrie forward like a child hesitant to enter a classroom on the first day of school.

"And I apparently wouldn't have missed it either," Wild Bill said, playing up Sally's soft grip on his coat sleeve.

"Not a Christmas movie fan, Bill?" Clive asked.

"Not especially," he admitted. "I'm more of a Western type

of film guy. But any chance to spend time with the good folks of this town is a fine time in my book. And a date night with this sweet lady here is always a plus." He gave Sally an endearing smile and placed a hand over hers, which was still firmly attached to his coat.

Once inside, enthusiastic moviegoers removed jackets and placed them on library tables that had been set up end to end for that purpose while clearing the center of the library for chairs.

"I want to sit with Clay!" Ben pointed to a row of chairs where his new friend had immediately found a seat. "Can I go? Please?" He turned a pleading look toward his mother.

"That's fine," Lauren said. "As long as I can see you. Let me have your coat." As soon as she pried it from his wiggling arms, he blasted off.

"I'm going straight for popcorn," Poppy said.

"I'm going with Poppy, okay?" Camille watched until Lauren nodded and then took off in search of the Christmas mix she'd sampled at Marge's store.

Mist eyed the popcorn counter, a clever conversion of the library's information area. Spotting the classic red-and-white containers, she remembered Millie's excitement when she'd ordered them as well as her delight that just about anything could be found on the internet.

"I think I'll pass on the popcorn," Sally said. "But I heard a rumor about hot mulled cider."

"Let's see if we can scout it out." Wild Bill, now with both arms free, placed a hand lightly on Sally's back and guided her toward the refreshment area.

Once the audience settled—a good twenty minutes past the scheduled time, but it was the first attempt at a movie night after all—the room grew dark, and the movie began. Soon only the voices of Maureen O'Hara, John Payne, Edmund Gwenn, and Natalie Wood graced the otherwise quiet library, although whispered comments could also be heard periodically along with the faint crunch of popcorn.

"I'm glad this is the original version."

"I just love little Natalie Wood! She's so sweet!"

"I've always wanted to see the Macy's parade in person."

"Kris Kringle must know a lot of languages!"

As the lights came up after the movie credits, a round of applause filled the room in praise of both the movie and the idea for the library to show it.

"Splendid in every way!" Andrew said to Millie on the way out. "You just may have to do this again."

"I don't see why not." Millie smiled as others departing waved to her. "It seems to have been a success."

Marge tapped Millie's arm as she passed by. "Not just a success but a huge success. And it wasn't just that Christmas popcorn."

Millie laughed. "Well, that giant bowl is certainly empty!"

"Maybe so, and I'm delighted it was enjoyed. But the heart of tonight was seeing the townsfolk come together to enjoy a nostalgic holiday evening. I even saw some people dropping donations into that container that's always by the checkout desk."

"I didn't expect that at all," Millie said, surprised. "The movie night was free on purpose. But it's wonderful. We use those funds for our outreach literacy program."

Mist and Michael, accompanied by most of the guests from the hotel, took turns thanking Millie for hosting the evening and then headed out. As the walk from the library to the hotel passed through the town park, they soon found themselves in front of the evergreen tree, now heavily laden with clear, round ornaments, each holding a variation of someone's hopes and dreams. The white lights on the tree's branches illuminated the wishes with an almost magical glow. Although it was too dark to read individual wishes within those ornaments with paper unfolded, they seemed to call out anyway.

"What a magnificent tree," Lauren said. She tucked her arm into Keith's as the children ran off to circle the tree in search of ornaments they'd filled and hung themselves.

"We added something earlier today," she whispered to Mist. "You got us thinking about that trip up the Mississippi. We thought it couldn't hurt to throw a wish up there with everyone else's."

"Wonderful," Justine said, having overheard. "You never know, right?"

True, Mist thought to herself. There was no way to know if most wishes would come true. But making them offered a chance for reflection, even the possibility of discovering a wish that always existed yet had remained undiscovered. The evergreen tree had become symbolic of the town's hopes and dreams as well as those of holiday visitors.

As the chill of the night began to creep through jackets, hats, and gloves, hotel guests continued on to the warmth of the hotel's front parlor and promise of hot chocolate and sweets—not that those were needed after the Christmas popcorn infusion—or to retire to their rooms for a peaceful night's sleep after the busy day and evening.

Chapter Ten

THE AIR WAS CHILLY IN SPITE OF BRIGHT SUNSHINE AS Mist stepped out of the hotel and started down the front walk. Her arms full with a delivery for Clive's gallery, she smiled and nodded to a car driving by, a local she recognized from meals at the café. There was hardly a soul in Timberton who didn't come to the Moonglow Café on occasion if not more often. Quite a few had come by that very morning for cinnamon french toast, herbed egg scramble, and fresh-squeezed orange juice.

As in any community, elderly or disabled residents sometimes faced challenges getting around. Mist had started a service, with the help of local volunteers, to deliver meals. The same volunteers also offered rides to the café. Often it was easier to have a meal at home, but occasionally it was nice to be able to enjoy the ambiance of the café itself as well as to have the camaraderie of sharing a meal with others.

Mist clutched the box of mini paintings she carried and turned in the direction of the gallery. She'd added a new design this year, something she tried to do every year. A recent drive she'd taken with Michael had led them through a forest area as a full moon rose over the landscape. She was pleased with the way this translated itself onto canvas, forming a design with soothing blues and greens, soft moonlight, and subtle touches of snow on the forest floor and branches. She'd titled the mini painting *Winter Forest*, and it had already proven to be popular.

Clive was busy with customers when she arrived, which was not surprising. His jewelry was always a hit during the holidays, just as it was at other times of the year. The Christmas ornaments he designed—originally for Betty, but now, at her insistence, available to others as well—were also in high demand. He never allowed the one he made for Betty each year to be sold that year, but it joined the collection when the next Christmas season rolled around.

Mist set the box of paintings on Clive's desk in the back of the shop. She'd managed to set aside three dozen of the four-by-four-inch paintings in assorted designs, knowing he would want a delivery for restocking on the holiday weekend. He always needed more for the last few days of Christmas shopping. The small, unique items made an easy gift.

"I see you have some new mini painting designs." Mist turned to see Clara holding two of the pottery mugs she'd admired at the hotel. Beyond her, she noted Andrew at the jewelry counter with Clive, pointing to something in the case. Both men sent a glance in Clara's direction.

"And I see you found the mugs," Mist said. "Did you see the petite round dishes too?" She casually guided Clara back toward the pottery display. "I'd like to get some for the hotel. Mix and match, I think."

"I saw those." Clara regarded the varying colors and shapes —some flatter, some deeper, all delightful. "Maybe we'll get a few. They'd be great for small servings of sauce on the side."

"Clive can ship any purchases home for you if that makes it easier to travel," Mist offered.

"What an excellent idea. I didn't even think of that!" Clara exclaimed. "I was trying to picture what I could fit in our suitcases. I'll pick some out now."

Mist left Clara to debate her pottery choices, excusing herself to return to the hotel. She stopped by Clive briefly to let him know the new mini paintings were waiting on his back desk.

"Thank you for keeping Clara occupied," Clive said, patting Mist on the shoulder. "That was a smooth move. Andrew picked out the sweetest necklace for her. I'll drop it by the hotel later."

"Just in time for dinner and cookie exchange extras, I imagine," Mist said with a teasing glint in her eye.

"Never would have occurred to me!" Clive laughed and moved on to help a new customer as Mist headed out.

THE TOWN PARK was quiet when Mist arrived. Only a soft flutter of snowflakes fell from the sky, and it appeared most of the townsfolk, those who weren't in small shops, looking for Christmas gifts, were tucked away in their homes. The tree had acquired more wishes since the day before, and Mist brushed light snow off a few in order to take a look. Some of the clear ornaments were filled with folded notes, holding secrets from those hoping their hidden status might make their wishes come true. Others were facing out, easily read, and they touched Mist's heart. "I wish my grandmother wasn't alone," one read. "I wish I could swim" on another. Several had simple, heartfelt phrases such as "peace" or "a joyful holiday" or "an end to poverty." One that appeared to be written by a child said, "I wish I had more books." Perhaps she and Millie, the librarian, could work on recognizing that handwriting and fulfill the wish.

Mist stepped back and observed the tree as a whole, its wish-bearing ornaments standing together as if whispering to the town. Perhaps this was the essence of the holiday project itself. It was a way to bring the community together in hopes of bettering their lives and the lives of others. Timberton was indeed a special town already. Anyone who lived there or visited could feel the magic in the air. But couldn't even a special town become more special?

As Mist pondered those thoughts, she could feel the wishes calling to her, calling to everyone who might listen. She felt a familiar hand slip around her waist, and she leaned her head against Michael's shoulder.

"I had a feeling I'd find you here," he said.

Mist smiled as he placed a soft kiss on her cheek, its warmth forming an enchanting sensation when mixed with the snow on her face. "How did you know?"

"For one thing, the kitchen was empty." Michael laughed before growing more serious. "And for another, I suspect these wishes call out to you."

"They do. And more show up all the time." Mist craned her neck, noting ornaments that Clayton had moved higher on the tree to allow others to be added on lower branches. "I love to check them each day."

"What do you wish for, Mist?"

"You know what my wish is, Michael. And it's already come true. It's for this life right here with you, with the Moon-glow Café, with the hotel, and with all the wonderful people of Timberton. This is the life I've always wished for, even before I knew it. And I'm so lucky to have it."

"I know that exact feeling," Michael said. He held Mist

close and admired the tree. "You know you can't make all these wishes come true even though I'm sure you'd like them to."

Mist nodded. "I know that. But it doesn't mean we can't help some come true, some of the ones not folded as secrets. Look at this one, for example." She slipped out of his embrace and took his hand, leading him to an ornament holding a wish for more books. "This is a child's writing. Maybe we could organize a drive for children's books and then distribute them. I'm going to talk to Millie about it."

"That's a great idea," Michael said.

Mist moved to another. "And this one about the grandmother being lonely. We have a few activities for seniors around town, but maybe we need an outreach program for those who have trouble getting to events."

"Another great idea. You are always filled with them. It's part of what makes you special."

Mist sighed. "That's kind of you to say, but making wishes come true isn't always that easy."

"You'll find a way," Michael said. "At least for some of these."

"*We'll* find a way."

Chapter Eleven

Mist had just settled into the kitchen to start dinner prep when the side door opened. A blast of cold air accompanied Betty's arrival. She removed her knit cap and gloves and ran a hand through her silver hair. She hung her jacket on a wall hook, poured herself a cup of coffee, and took a seat at the center island where Mist was chopping vegetables.

"Dinner already?" Betty chuckled. "It's not quite lunchtime yet." She pulled a small bag of caramels out of her pocket and placed it on the counter, a clear indication she'd been to Marge's.

Mist contemplated teasing Betty with a quick comment about the virtue of being prepared but opted for an easier answer. "I may have an errand to run this afternoon."

"Is there anything I can do for you while you're out?"

"Just enjoy your annual cookie exchange this afternoon," Mist pointed out. "Relax and have fun with that. You look forward to it all year."

Betty grinned. "Very true! There's no better combination of sugar and gossip to be found!"

Mist laughed, both at Betty's enthusiasm and the truth she spoke. "Everything the participants need is on the buffet: containers, covers, and notepaper and pens in case they wish to make notes."

"Thanks for setting that up." Betty lifted her coffee cup to her lips but set it down, letting it cool. "I can't wait to see what everyone's bringing this year."

"Whatever they bring will be delicious." Mist was always impressed with the creative treats that appeared for the event. Between cookies, nut bars, truffles, brownies, and a dozen other delicious sweets, there was something for everyone.

"I stopped by the wishing tree on my way back from Marge's," Betty said. "Some of the ornaments with wishes are hung low to the ground. Do you think those are from children?"

Mist nodded. "I'm sure they are. It was a great idea of Millie's to keep empty ornaments, paper, and pencils on a low table at the library so children could write their wishes and put them on the tree themselves."

"So the level of the ornaments on the tree might be a hint about whether they're from children or adults."

"Possibly," Mist said, smiling. "I suppose adults might randomly place them higher or lower. But I imagine they're more likely to reach up."

"I love that some wishes are hidden inside folded paper while others are facing out, able to be read." Betty pulled a caramel from a pocket, unwrapped it, and popped it in her mouth.

"Yes," Mist said. "I happened to see a new wish this morning on my way back from the gallery that I think is from a guest here."

"Really?" Betty raised an eyebrow. "Which guest?"

"Camille."

"Ah, Camille, such a sweet girl," Betty said. "What makes you think it's from her?"

"Several things. I know she and her mother went to the library yesterday." Mist said a silent thank-you for the program that Millie offered for hotel guests to be able to check out books and have the hotel return them after they left. "She would have had a chance to fill one out then. Or she might have at the movie night last night."

"And? What else?"

"She also asked this morning if we could put on some music that had violins." Mist smiled, thinking about how excited Camille became when she said yes. "Her eyes lit up when I told her we had Lindsey Stirling's *Snow Waltz* album."

"So... what is the wish?" Betty leaned forward, intrigued.

"The wish on the tree is to be able to play a violin. It just happens to hang around Camille's height."

"Aha." Betty took a sip of coffee. "You may have a future as an amateur sleuth."

Mist smiled but didn't comment. Many wishes would never be fulfilled. After all, this was the nature of life. But there was a chance she could have a hand in this one, thanks to a phone call Michael was making.

"Any other clever detective work you've managed?"

"Maybe one other..." Mist let the sentence trail off as she pondered a plan she hoped would come together. "I need to talk to Clayton about that one."

"Ah." Betty nodded. "This is the part where you say 'It takes a village.'"

Unable to resist the cue, Mist whispered, "It takes a village."

Betty took in the ingredients spread out in front of Mist and tried to mentally combine them. "Let me venture a guess. Chicken Pot Pie."

Mist nodded. "Yes. Hot and filling for a cold winter night."

"And the other one?" Betty pointed to a second baking tray.

"A roasted veggie quinoa casserole," Mist explained. "In case we have diners tonight who don't eat chicken. It will make a good side dish even for those who do."

Michael stepped into the kitchen and snuck a kiss onto Mist's cheek as she began rolling out the dough for a crust.

"Beware of flour," Mist said teasingly.

Michael laughed. "That's okay. It just means I'm getting some of my dinner in advance. But I came in to tell you I reached David, the music professor I know at the university. Our mission is a go, should you choose to accept it."

Betty's eyebrows lifted. "Such a mystery. Maybe you two are spies and I simply never knew it."

"Nothing quite that exciting." Michael laughed.

"Yet very exciting for a young child with musical aspirations." Mist set the dough aside and began to dice potatoes.

"Aha, the plot thickens," Betty quipped.

"I can run up there alone if you want," Michael offered.

Mist shook her head. "I'd like to go if I can have an hour to finish dinner prep. I still have"—she surveyed the counter and then peered in the refrigerator—"yes, that will be enough time."

"Then I'll be back." Michael gave her another kiss and left her to her tasks.

Mist finished both casseroles within the hour, accepting—with only the slightest hesitation—help from Betty, who offered to cover and store the casseroles so Mist could get on her way. Satisfied that all was under control for dinner that evening, she cleaned up the kitchen and then double-checked the cookie-exchange setup in the café.

Passing through the lobby on her way out to meet Michael, Mist grabbed a coat and then spied the professor and Poppy in the front parlor, absorbed in a book likely pulled from one of the tall bookcases. They sat side by side, the professor with his eyes closed, Poppy doing a rather dramatic reading. Mist leaned in the arched doorway and listened. Poppy soon looked up.

"What are you and your uncle reading?" Mist said. With one person reading and one listening, the professor and Poppy were, in reality, both reading. "Would this happen to be *A Christmas Carol* again?" The professor's love for the Dickens classic was well-known.

"Not this time," the professor said, his eyes still closed. "Tell our dear Mist the selections we have, Poppy."

"We have quite a few short stories," Poppy said. She picked up a stack of books beside her and shuffled through them: "*The Gift of the Magi*, by O. Henry, *The Fir-Tree*, by Hans Christian Anderson, *A Child's Christmas in Wales*, by Dylan Thomas, and *The Cricket on the Hearth*."

"Now there's your Dickens!" the professor exclaimed, opening his eyes and noting Mist's coat. "And where are you off to?"

"A secret mission," Mist said, seeing Michael's car through the window. With a hint of a grin, she left them to enjoy their reading and headed out.

Chapter Twelve

Mist looked out the window as Michael turned in to the university parking lot and pulled into a spot. Although she'd been out of Timberton many times over the years, especially once she started seeing Michael, it still amazed her to see how different the surroundings were. She was familiar with this type of environment, having grown up in California and studied art at UC Santa Cruz. But after a decade in Timberton, she'd grown used to the small community and come to love the quiet mountain town. The two-lane roads, quaint buildings, unique individually owned shops, and close community were comforting. Timberton was home.

Still, she was grateful that Maisie and Betty had encouraged her to accompany Michael up to the university's music department. Breakfast was finished, much of dinner prep had been accomplished while guests were having breakfast, and Mist would be back in time to finish preparing the evening meal. Betty's annual cookie exchange, to be held later that afternoon, was one activity that Betty managed herself. The hotelkeeper had been hosting the event for years, long before

Mist came to Timberton. Mist loved coordinating containers for the participants to fill with sweets, coming up with original ideas each year. But otherwise, she stood aside and let Betty enjoy the spotlight.

Stepping out of the car, she adjusted the hand-knit hat that she'd found at Second Hand Sally's a few months before and pulled her wool coat around her. Although it was her habit to wear a burgundy cape for short errands in Timberton, the coat was warmer for trips out of town. As with most of her clothes, at least the ones she didn't make herself, she'd found the deep green coat at a thrift shop. On a whim, she'd gathered mismatched vintage buttons and replaced the existing ones with various styles, each buttonhole gaining a distinguished companion: a Czech glass button with turquoise and gold accents, a pewter circle with a Celtic knot, a ceramic square with petite aspen leaves, an olive wood filigree button resembling a spool of thread, and others with unique styles and shapes.

Mist walked with Michael, his arm around her shoulders, light snowflakes falling as they approached their destination. The university's music department was housed in a stately structure as solid as the quality of instruction and as welcoming as the kindness of the faculty. The trip there today exemplified that kindness in the willingness of a fellow faculty member to meet on campus just two days before Christmas, during the holiday break from classes. Once the instructor who ran the instrument outreach program heard about Mist's idea, he was happy to help out.

The door to the music building was unlocked, just as the music instructor said it would be. As opposed to the quiet that Mist expected to hear once inside, soft voices flowed through the hall in exquisite harmony. This was soon explained by a flyer on a bulletin board announcing a performance of holiday choral music that evening.

"Do you hear that?" Mist whispered as if a loud voice in the hallway would interfere with the rehearsal. She took Michael's hand and gently pulled him in the direction of the music. "'Carol of the Bells,'" she said when they reached the doorway. "Just listen." With an impish expression, she eased the door open a fraction of an inch, just enough to hear the voices more clearly. "It's beautiful. I've always adored this one."

"We're about twenty minutes early," Michael said, checking the time. "We could slip inside the room for a bit."

Mist's face brightened. "Really? I don't want to interrupt, but that would be wonderful!"

Michael put a finger up to his lips and reached for the door handle, his fingers brushing across Mist's as she let go. They tiptoed in and took places on one of three long benches that stretched across the top of the large room, which resembled more of a lecture hall than a classroom. Mist immediately felt as if she were back in her university classes, finding it almost magical how a step into a room could trigger memories from long ago and make them feel like they were just the other day.

The chorus moved on to a rendition of "The Little Drummer Boy" followed by "O Come, All Ye Faithful." Michael reached for Mist's hand, and their fingers intertwined. Mist marveled at the unexpected interlude in the midst of the busy holiday hotel activities. Timberton felt like another world, as if they'd just stepped into a parallel universe that they would just as quickly step out of a few hours later.

Mist tapped Michael's arm and gestured to a clock on the wall. Realizing it was time to meet the instructor they'd spoken with earlier, they slipped out of the rehearsal unnoticed. Michael led them to a stairwell, and Mist followed him down to a lower level.

They passed small practice rooms with pianos, empty now that students were on break. At the end of the hallway, an open door signaled their arrival, and Michael soon was shaking hands with David Woodson, a gentleman who looked to be in his late forties.

Once all introductions were complete, Mist looked around in awe. Metal shelves lined the walls of the room, which was smaller than a classroom yet larger than a storage room. Instruments lay organized by type—woodwinds in one area, strings in another, percussion in yet another. Tags hung from many of them, noting where the instrument had come from and any specifics to the item. Again, the feeling of being in another place and time passed through her. Had she just served breakfast a few hours before this? Would she be welcoming guests to dinner in just a few hours?

"I can't tell you how grateful I am—we are—for your help," Mist said. "This child is going to be so excited."

"That's exactly what this program is for," David said. "It's an exchange I started about ten years ago." He reached up to one shelf and pulled a hard case down. "People donate instruments, and we pass them on to others who can use them, especially children when we can. It's important for their love of music to be nurtured."

"That's wonderful," Mist said. "It could make the whole difference of a child pursuing a dream or letting it go."

"Exactly." David opened the case and took out a violin. Mist caught her breath as if the instrument had just been conjured up by magic. "You said the child is about eight years old?"

"Yes," Mist said. "And her mother measured her arm, as you suggested. It's just a touch under twenty inches." Mist thought it clever that Lauren had suggested measuring it for a new jacket to avoid giving away the surprise.

David nodded. "Then this will be right for her. It's a half-size violin, appropriate for her age and arm length. It's not new, of course, but it's in rather nice condition."

"She'll be thrilled," Michael said.

"We're so grateful," Mist added.

David smiled. "Always encouraging to see a child discovering the world of music." He gently placed the violin and accompanying bow back in the case and handed it to Mist. After thanking him, Mist and Michael headed for the parking lot, brushed snow off the windows of the car, and started back to the hotel.

"I'm so glad Camille's parents were okay with this," Mist said. "I wasn't sure how they'd take the suggestion. But when I explained it wasn't charity or an obligation or anything other than a simple program aimed at providing instruments to those who would enjoy them, they were fine."

Michael nodded, keeping his eyes on the road. "Another little Christmas miracle in Timberton, I suppose."

"Helping a child's wish come true..." Mist smiled. "Yes, I suppose that's the best kind of miracle."

Chapter Thirteen

As expected, Mist entered the hotel to find cheerful conversation and laughter flowing from the café. A record number of cookie-exchange participants filled the room, many holding glass mugs of wassail while standing in small clusters around the extended table area that had been formed by pushing tables together end to end. Serving plates, trays, and baskets were nearly empty, each person having filled a wooden tray with assorted cookies and other sweet treats.

Betty looked the part of the ultimate holiday hostess as she moved around the room in a soft black A-line skirt, white blouse, and red sweater-vest with appliquéd snowmen and rhinestones. She'd added a reindeer antler headband to liven up the outfit as well as sparkly snowman earrings.

"We've had the most marvelous assortment of goodies today," Betty said as she welcomed Mist back. "Marge brought Christmas popcorn from the candy store, Sally made chocolate-dipped orange butter cookies, Glenda showed up with salted peanut cookies, and..." Her voice trailed off as she glanced at the table, reminding herself of the extravagant spread of sugar-laden treats.

"It looks like I see some gingerbread in the mix," Mist noted as she stepped closer to the table.

"Gingerbread kiss cookies," Betty said. "Millie dropped those off but had to get back to the library. But look at all this..." Betty pointed to other containers as she circled the table. "Cranberry white chocolate bars, pecan fingers, caramel apple cookies, chocolate fudge, and so many more!"

"The town's going to be on a sugar high until the new year," Sally said, adding a date nut torte square to her assortment. A strand of lights flashed on and off around the base of a Santa hat she wore. "And I love these wooden trays and the fascinating wrap, Mist!"

Mist smiled. Searching for reusable containers for Betty's annual cookie exchange was one of her joys for the holiday season. It gave the participants something to keep as opposed to the cookies and treats, which were destined to disappear quickly. This year, the small wooden trays she'd found were perfect. They had just enough of a lip to hold the treats in. She'd been equally delighted to find sustainable cloth wrapping for covers, which she'd learned about from the owner of an amazing catering company. The combination of cotton, beeswax, plant oil, and tree resin allowed the wrap to be reused and eventually composted.

"Was your errand with Michael successful?" Betty asked. She chose her words cautiously even though she knew the Coopers had left to browse local shops.

"Very much so," Mist said. "Michael's dropping it off at home to keep it out of the way until Christmas morning."

"Good idea," Betty said as she moved a tray of almond bars closer to a plate of red velvet cake cookies. "It'll be a wonderful surprise for that sweet little girl on Christmas morning."

Mist eyed the treats with a sudden longing as Betty straightened those left on the table. She'd never been one to be especially fond of sugary desserts, but they seemed to appeal to her this season. All a part of holiday magic, she mused. Perhaps she'd indulge in a cookie or two, even a mug of hot chocolate, later in the evening in the front parlor. It would be delightful to mingle with others after dinner.

At thoughts of the evening meal, she excused herself and moved into the kitchen, leaving Betty to enjoy the remainder of her cookie-exchange time. She checked the covered casseroles that had been prepared earlier, noting that they were ready to slip into the oven at the appropriate time, and then set about preparing side dishes. With the kitchen to herself, she soon had the makings of a mixed green salad rinsed and ready to toss together just before being served. She stirred the cucumber salad that had been marinating since the morning, recovered it, and placed it back in the refrigerator. After filling and covering a large oval basket with multigrain wheat rolls, she stepped back and did a mental inventory of the meal to be served. Yes, it was set.

"That was delightful," Betty exclaimed once the last participant had left, armed with sweets like all the rest. She dropped onto a chair at the center island and leaned on the counter with both arms. "And exhausting. I put a tray of extra cookies out in the lobby—high enough that Ben and Clay Jr. won't be able to grab them on their own."

"Your cookie exchange is always a success."

"It's not hard to have a good time when surrounded by sugary treats. I don't suppose the wassail hurt either, not after a few people added a touch of rum." Betty chuckled.

"I'm sure it didn't!" Mist grinned.

"What can I help you with?" Betty asked, although her expression couldn't hide her fatigue.

"Nothing," Mist said. "Everything is under control. Most of it was prepared before we even ran the errand earlier. Why don't you get some rest before dinner? Just pop out to have something to eat when you're ready. Maisie is coming by to help serve."

"You know, I do think I'll rest for a bit." Betty stood and started for the door to the back hallway. "But don't be afraid to call if you need help."

Maisie showed up in time to set up the café tables for dinner and arrange the serving dishes on the buffet. As with every evening, folks wandered in to enjoy the food and have a chance to visit with each other. Clive, never one to miss a meal, showed up after closing the gallery. Betty, rejuvenated from a nap, joined him.

After appetites were satisfied, the crowd either dispersed to their own homes or, if hotel guests, moved to the front parlor. Some guests set about making cranberry and popcorn garlands while others worked at a craft table or simply relaxed in front of the fire. Michael, as always, settled into his usual spot, book in hand.

With the day's activity behind her, Mist made herself a mug of peppermint tea and slipped through the kitchen's back door and into the hallway, following it to the small room she kept for herself. As she entered the room, she smiled at the vase of ivory roses, red cyclamen, and greenery that Maisie had nudged her to take. She wouldn't have thought to make this for herself, but there'd been extra flowers and greenery when they finished the café arrangements, and she was glad now that Maisie had suggested it.

Setting her tea down on a side table, she arranged the paints she needed and sat in front of the custom frame Clive had built for her years ago. The clever structure with numerous brackets and clips held a handful of the four-by-four canvases she used for her mini paintings. Knowing they were especially in demand during the holidays, she kept that frame full of blank canvases throughout the fall. Now, having delivered the final pre-Christmas batch to Clive's gallery, she turned to her favorite painting project of the season: mini paintings for the hotel guests.

The images for the paintings were often a mystery to her until she began painting, but this year she'd had an idea of what she wanted, and now she felt sure. Sorting through her paints, she chose deep sea green, tawny brown, and two shades of blue, knowing she would also add tiny accents of metallic gold and silver.

Mist sat back and reached for her tea, taking a sip of the soothing, minty beverage. Then she focused her eyes on the multifaceted easel as her imagination played with the size and shape of the blank canvases. Slowly she let the images in her mind fit into those spaces, filling them invisibly. Once content that the ethereal outlines were established, she set her tea down, picked up her brush, and started in.

Chapter Fourteen

Breakfast on Christmas Eve was always a casual, light meal, planned that way given the large feast that would be offered that evening. Thus, guests arrived downstairs on the last morning before Christmas to find Mist opening the café with an assortment of baked goods, fresh fruit, and homemade granola and toppings laid out on the buffet. A separate area for beverages offered a variety of juices as well as coffee, tea, and hot chocolate.

"Banana bread!" Justine exclaimed, noting a choice between some with nuts and some without. "A slice with walnuts along with a chilled glass of orange juice sounds perfect to me."

"And coffee, of course," Randall said, helping himself to a cinnamon roll.

"Yes," Justine agreed. "Definitely coffee."

"Or tea," the professor quipped, stepping up to survey the selections. He turned to his niece, who was just behind him, and gestured to another tray. "These must be for you, my dear."

Poppy nudged her uncle's arm playfully as she regarded a

mountain of lemon poppy seed muffins. "I doubt they're *all* for me, but I do think one must be." She added a muffin to a plate of fresh strawberries and followed the professor to a table. Soon joined by others, festive conversation flowed through the room. All felt some degree of anticipation with Christmas the next day.

"Are you sure Santa knows where we're staying?" Ben asked. He pushed a cinnamon scone across his plate, accompanying it with engine noises.

"I'm certain," Lauren said, gently parking the scone.

"Santa knows everything," Camille said matter-of-factly.

Mist checked the buffet and strolled around the room, making sure no one needed anything before returning to the kitchen, where morning cleanup and dinner preparations were alternating with remarkable efficiency. With Christmas Eve dinner being the most extravagant meal of the year, even with calculated planning, it took the majority of the day to prepare the feast.

As guests finished their breakfasts, a roaring fire in the front parlor's fireplace beckoned, and many decided to follow the promise of warmth into the main room to relax. Michael sat in his favorite armchair and lifted a book off a side table, where he'd left it the evening before. Andrew and the professor began a game of chess. The Coopers chose to go out for a winter drive, bundling their children up in jackets, hats, and gloves before departing.

Hollister passed through the lobby with Bacon, pausing to allow the sweet dog to enjoy some affectionate pats on the head on their way out for a walk. Randall perused the bookshelves, and Justine took a seat on the couch.

Clara took advantage of Andrew being occupied to sneak out to Marge's to buy Andrew sweets to put under the tree, grateful some of the town businesses would be open a half day.

Poppy, tempted by the lure of Marge's shop, asked to tag along. Both she and Clara agreed that a visit to the evergreen tree in the park to ponder the wishes would be a good stop while out and about.

The casual, relaxing afternoon for most was matched by a busy though cheerful afternoon in the kitchen. The familiar sounds of food prep filled the room, adding percussive accompaniment to Mist, Maisie, and Betty's cheerful work. The Christmas Eve dinner was always special at the Timberton Hotel, and the atmosphere in the kitchen was especially joyful. Betty hummed along with Dean Martin's "Winter Wonderland" as she whisked a vinaigrette dressing. Maisie tapped a paring knife lightly against a cutting board as she chopped parsley for garnishes. And Mist clinked bowls against each other as she rearranged the refrigerator in an attempt to find space for a tray of seasoned root vegetables. Even with the extra refrigerator downstairs filled with prepared dishes, the large kitchen fridge resembled a culinary jigsaw puzzle.

"It'll be a lovely dinner tonight," Betty said, smiling.

"It always is," Maisie agreed. "We all look forward to it, the townsfolk and your hotel guests. And those who travel from surrounding towns to enjoy it."

"She's right," Betty said. "All your meals are special, but the one on Christmas Eve is the most special of all."

"*Our* meals," Mist clarified. "Looking around this kitchen, I see a team effort. I could never do this alone, not with as many guests as we now have for the meal. Especially now that we have two seatings."

The café had offered two seatings several years before when the town held a Yuletide festival. With the popularity of the Christmas Eve dinner, it was decided that this should be a regular arrangement. The extra work would be worth it to avoid turning people away. Guests and many of the townsfolk would attend the second seating. The earlier time allowed visiting diners and local overflow to enjoy the festive meal.

Mist turned back from the refrigerator and reached into a basket on the counter, pulling out garlic to add to the root vegetables later when they slid into the oven. Maisie, having finished with the parsley, passed her the cutting board. As Mist prepared to pull cloves off the bulb, she suddenly dropped the garlic. In a move most unusual for her, she wrinkled her nose.

"I think something's wrong with the garlic." Mist frowned, pushed it aside, and retrieved another bulb from the basket. Again, she frowned.

"What's the matter?" Maisie reached across the kitchen island and picked up both garlic bulbs. She smelled one, then the other. "I think these are fine." She handed them back to Mist.

Betty moved over to stand by Maisie and looked at Mist and the garlic. "What's wrong with them?"

Mist shook her head as if trying to clear her senses. "They just don't smell right. Too strong, don't you think? Garlic doesn't smell this strong. It's not even peeled." She looked up at Betty and Maisie, who exchanged glances, both with eyebrows raised. They turned back to Mist, smiling, but didn't say anything.

"What?" Mist picked up the garlic and headed to the trash.

Betty intercepted and gently took the garlic from her. "I'll peel the cloves, don't worry."

"But..." Mist stood puzzled. "But we can't use ingredients that aren't fresh."

"There's nothing wrong with the garlic," Maisie said gently.

"It's absolutely fine," Betty said, setting the garlic down.

Mist looked from one face to another, puzzled at the two women's behavior. But as Maisie gently placed her hand on her stomach, an expression of wonder took over Mist's face. She quickly sat down on one of the counter stools and looked back and forth between Maisie and Betty.

"You really think so?"

Maisie and Betty both nodded.

"It's the most reasonable explanation," Betty said, barely able to keep her excitement contained.

Maisie grinned. "I suspect we're both in for an exciting year ahead. With *two* summer miracles."

"Two summer miracles...," Mist repeated, too astonished to say anything else. Could Betty and Maisie be right?

As all three started to continue the conversation, the kitchen door opened, and Michael walked in. "What's up in here?"

"Nothing!" all three women said quickly. Michael stopped, took in the odd expressions, and did an about-face. "Okay then!" he called over his shoulder, exiting as quickly as he'd entered.

"Thank you," Mist said to Maisie and Betty after Michael was gone.

"All in good time," Betty said.

"Yes," Maisie agreed.

Mist stood up. "And now we have a wonderful meal to finish preparing."

"I'd better do the garlic," Betty said, laughing.

Mist grinned. "Yes, I think that's an excellent idea."

Chapter Fifteen

As was her habit, Mist stood alone in the café before opening the doors for the eager dinner crowd. Those waiting in the lobby and front parlor had been treated to appetizers, pleasant holiday music, and beverages of their choice. In contrast to the cheerful atmosphere the guests enjoyed, Mist took in the ambiance of the café's low lights, the flicker of votive candles on the table, the freshness of flower arrangements, and the splendor of the elegant buffet ready to serve a delicious meal. These were special moments to her, a time to breathe her own wish into the room, that of hope for a joyous evening to be shared by all, for special memories to be made, for the Moonglow Café to offer what it always hoped to offer: peace.

When it was time, Mist stepped into the kitchen where Betty and Maisie stood ready to help serve the meal. Seeing Mist smile and nod her head, they began to carry serving dishes to the buffet, which was soon overflowing with this year's Christmas Eve dinner fare. Mist opened the doors to the café, much to the delight of those waiting, who cheered and clapped.

As the guests entered, Mist greeted each one, welcoming them to another year's celebration.

The annual Christmas Eve dinner required careful timing, especially since the café had gone to two seatings. But the first set of reservations went off without a hitch—much thanks to Betty, Clive, and Maisie's help in the kitchen—and the café moved on to the second sitting, the one that included the hotel guests and many locals.

"You look like a princess, Mist!" Clara said upon entering, admiring Mist's flowing hunter green dress with an ivory floral design along one sleeve and around the bottom of the skirt. Mist had been thrilled to see it come into Sally's thrift shop. A mother-of-pearl barrette, vintage rhinestone earrings, and silver ballet slippers had been all that was needed to dress it up.

"Thank you, Clara. You look lovely yourself." Mist noted that both Clara and Andrew had dressed up for the evening, Clara in a bright red dress and green silk jacket and Andrew in a suit.

"Really," Clara exclaimed just before stepping away. "You're positively glowing!"

Mist stifled a laugh and then grinned, certain the coming year held a change of the most remarkable kind.

The professor and Poppy arrived next, soon followed by the other hotel guests and many local townsfolk. Clayton brought Clay Jr. and his parents, Wild Bill and Sally arrived together, which most everyone now expected, and Millie arrived to a round of applause that astonished her, a thank-you for the movie night she'd arranged for the town. Mist was pleased to see Duffy arrive and take a seat by the professor. And she was especially delighted to see Hollister slip in quietly, accompanied by Bacon, who took a surreptitious place under the table.

"Don't be shy, everyone," Clive called from the kitchen

door once the café was full. He gestured to the buffet. "I can't eat all that myself!"

"We'd better help you out then," Wild Bill said, standing up and reaching for Sally's hand.

"Count us in too!" Andrew motioned to the other hotel guests, who followed his lead to the buffet.

With plates laden with brisket with fennel and rosemary, cranberry gnocchi with butter sauce, and side dishes ranging from brussels sprouts to butternut squash to glazed carrots, not to mention Parmesan rolls, it was a wonder anyone had room for the individual spiced pear soufflés when they arrived after the main meal.

"Where am I going to put this?" Lauren mused aloud, admiring the tiny mint leaf garnishing the top of her soufflé.

"In your stomach," Ben piped up, obviously voicing the correct answer to the question, rhetorical though it had been. Satisfied that he'd solved his mother's dilemma, he took a bite of his own dessert and grinned. "I like this. Can we have it every night at home?"

"Good luck with that," Justine said, leaning toward Lauren from the next table. "I've tried to make soufflés a few times without much success. But this is delicious enough to try again."

Mist circled the room, announcing that coffee was available in the café itself or could be picked up in the lobby and taken to the front parlor, where both guests and townsfolk were welcome to relax and visit. Most everyone chose to move over to enjoy the Christmas tree, warm fire, and heartfelt camaraderie after the remarkable meal.

Randall tried his hand at playing a few traditional carols at the hotel's spinet piano. Despite offering a disclaimer that he hadn't played in years, he was remarkably good, so much so that the crowd was soon singing along to "Hark the Herald Angels Sing" and "Joy to the World."

Clive, per tradition started many years before, guided Betty to the Christmas tree, where he reached around to a very back branch. Pulling a small ornament forward, he presented her with this year's creation, an elegant silver star with his signature touch of tiny Yogo sapphires at each point.

"It's beautiful, Clive!" Betty exclaimed. "Every one of your custom designs is exquisite. This will be a wonderful addition to the collection."

"But can you name them all?" Clara asked.

"I certainly can," Betty announced. "There's a wreath, a snowflake, a stocking, a pair of bells, a reindeer, a trio of candles, a Christmas tree, and"—she tapped a finger against her forehead, digging deep into her memory—"and the word *joy* in a lovely script. That was last year."

"Quite impressive," the professor said. "And what will it be next year?" He turned to Clive, attempting to pry a secret from him.

"I never know until I sit down to make it," Clive explained. "That goes for all my jewelry."

Randall played a few more carols, now softer as a calm settled over the room. Lauren and Keith shuffled the children off to bed, telling them morning would arrive sooner if they went to sleep now. Little by little, the festivities wound down. Betty retreated to the kitchen but not before Clive caught her for a brief kiss under the mistletoe. In the end, only Mist and Michael remained, Michael seated before the fire, Mist sweetly sitting on his lap.

"A lovely Christmas Eve, as always." Michael drew her close for a kiss.

"The loveliest ever," Mist whispered.

"I'm not sure about that," Michael said. "I recall a pretty special Christmas Eve last year."

Mist smiled. "True. Our Christmas Eve wedding was an evening we'll never forget. But... this may be another one you'll always remember."

"And why is that?" Michael asked so casually that Mist almost laughed out loud, knowing he couldn't possibly anticipate what she was about to tell him.

Mist leaned close to Michael's ear and began to whisper, and as she did, his eyes grew wide, matched only by an even wider smile.

"Really? When?"

"Yes, really." Mist tousled Michael's hair, charmed by his sudden inability to form complete sentences. "I'm guessing maybe July. We'll find out more."

Michael pulled her close, and she nestled her head against his neck. "Why don't you come home and rest? Tomorrow will be busy. Christmas morning always is."

Mist stifled a yawn. The idea was tempting, but there was still one more task to attend to, one that was her tradition each Christmas Eve.

"Ah," Michael said as if reading her mind. "The mini paintings."

"Yes, the mini paintings." Mist stood and leaned over to give Michael another kiss. "Just a few last-minute details. Go on home. I won't be long."

And with that, the hotel eased into the night, the guest rooms silent, the café and front parlor filled with memories of a joy-filled evening, and one peaceful artist settled in front of her easel to add final touches to miniature canvases that would find new homes on Christmas morning.

Chapter Sixteen

It was no surprise to Mist that Ben and Camille were the first ones to descend in the morning, tiptoeing down the stairway and scooting up close to the Christmas tree. Several packages had appeared beneath the branches overnight, as expected. Lauren and Keith had sent a box in advance, which had been set aside, out of sight, awaiting their arrival. Justine and Randall had each placed gifts under the tree the night before when the other wasn't looking. Clara and Andrew had agreed not to exchange gifts, yet Clara had picked up treats from Marge's candy shop for Andrew, and Mist knew Andrew's sly behavior at Clive's had resulted in a small package tucked in with the others. The professor had also slipped several things under the tree for Poppy.

Although the lure of gifts was strong, breakfast was first. Christmas Day was one morning when the meal was only offered to those staying at the hotel.

Guests arrived in the café to upbeat renditions of Christmas carols flowing from the sound system. "Joy to the World" was soon followed by "Good King Wenceslas," "Have a

Holly Jolly Christmas," and "Jingle Bell Rock." Clive, chipper and dashing in a Santa hat, hummed along with the music as he delivered pancakes—regular, blueberry, or chocolate chip—to tables by request. A medley of fresh berries accompanied an herbed frittata and seasoned home fries on the buffet. Mist made the rounds with a pitcher of fresh-squeezed orange juice. Betty circled around other tables with a carafe of Mist's legendary Java Love, stopping briefly to tease the professor with a mock attempt to refill his tea with coffee.

Breakfast was lively but quickly over as the presents in the front parlor seemed to extend nothing short of a magnetic pull. Ben was soon parked in front of the tree, eager to unwrap gifts Santa had dropped off in the middle of the night. Camille and Poppy found places nearby, and the adults weren't far behind.

"Clive," Betty suggested, "why don't you do the honors?"

Clive adjusted his Santa hat and rubbed his hands together. "Don't mind if I do!" He surveyed the packages and chose one each for Ben and Camille to start with. As they unwrapped those, he distributed others around the room. "Oohs" and "aahs" mixed with the sound of crinkling paper as presents were opened.

Clara kissed Andrew's cheek, delighted with the Yogo sapphire pendant he'd picked out at the gallery. "You did a beautiful job on this, Clive!"

"I thank you kindly." Clive took a small bow, which was followed by good-natured laughter.

The other adults were thrilled with thoughtful gifts they'd managed to coordinate: Justine and Randall's were brought in with their luggage, and Lauren and Keith's were shipped ahead.

When the gifts had all been opened, Mist took Clive's

place in front of the tree. She gently pulled her small packages from between the branches, taking care not to disturb ornaments, and faced the room, checking the handmade name tags she'd placed on each gift.

"We have a tradition here at the Timberton Hotel," she explained to the first-time guests. "We want you to have something to take home with you as a remembrance of your Christmas holiday here." Without further ado, she distributed the small packages around the room. "It's fine to open them together," she added as they looked around, each wondering who might open theirs first.

One by one, the stenciled paper and raffia fell away, and each guest held up the miniature canvas Mist had painted for them.

"It's the tree from the town park," Poppy said, holding hers up for others to see. "With a scrapbook beneath it!"

"To record your adventures here in the US," Mist said.

"My hopes and dreams for this semester." Poppy turned the painting toward her. "And there's a pen in the tree for an ornament. Brilliant!"

Clara and Andrew admired theirs. "Two suitcases, how clever," Clara exclaimed.

"To represent whatever future travel you wish to take," Mist said.

"I love all the books on our tree!" Justine turned to Randall. "We have the makings of our reading binge right here!"

"Ours is wonderful too," Lauren said, admiring the painting she and Keith had just opened. "How clever to put a paddle boat ornament on the tree!"

Keith nodded. "Now when we're ready, you can just take it off the tree and start sailing up the Mississippi."

"Mine has a fire truck under the tree!" Ben said. "I'm going to drive it when I'm older."

"And mine has a violin," Camille said, equally excited.

"You can play it when you grow up," Ben suggested.

Camille faced Ben, her expression serious. "Ben, I can't play this one. This *represents* one I'll play. Like yours *represents* one you might drive in the future."

"What does that mean?" Ben looked to Camille for an explanation, but Poppy spoke first.

"It means the painting reminds you of something you hope for the future."

Mist smiled. Poppy's explanation was something she might say herself.

"A long time from now?" Ben asked. His young brow furrowed as he contemplated this.

Poppy smiled. "Well, you do need to be old enough to drive."

"Or maybe not," an unexpected voice said.

Everyone turned to see Clayton standing in the archway to the room, Clay Jr. by his side. Both were dressed in fireman's gear, Clay Jr. wearing a child-sized version of his father's uniform. Maisie stood beside them, a similar outfit in her arms.

Ben's eyes grew wide as surprised murmurs circled the room. He jumped up, Poppy catching his hastily abandoned painting as he ran over to Maisie and let her help him into the yellow slicker and red fireman's hat. Lauren grabbed her phone and followed the boys as they ran outside where Timberton's shiny red fire truck stood waiting in front of the hotel. Lauren managed a few photos of the boys standing in front of the truck —a tricky endeavor as the boys could barely stand still.

With other hotel guests watching from the window and some local townsfolk enjoying a roadside view, Clayton started the fire truck up with a noisy rumble and headed off on a slow trip around the town outskirts. It would forever remain a mystery whether Clayton let Ben sit on his lap and hold the steering wheel for a short block on a side road, but Ben returned to the hotel with a grin that stretched from ear to ear. When asked if he got to drive, Ben said it was a secret for firemen only.

"You probably could have gone," Lauren said to Camille as she stepped back inside, pleased with the photos she'd taken.

Camille shook her head, calm and smiling. "It was better for Ben to go on his own. That was a great Christmas surprise for him. He's always talking about fire trucks."

"Do you think he'll stop talking about them now?" Keith asked, already knowing the answer.

Lauren and Camille both laughed. "Not a chance," Lauren said.

Mist stepped forward, having observed the scene quietly. Lauren and Keith clasped hands, watching her closely.

"Camille," Mist said, "we all know that wishes don't always come true. Sometimes they're just wishes, and that's fine. Wishes keep our spirits alive."

Camille nodded, looking again at her painting. "It's fun to have them even if they're always just wishes."

"I agree." Mist crouched down in order to be at eye level with the young girl. "However, sometimes wishes *are* meant to come true. It's one of life's surprises, the unexpected. Like your brother getting to ride in a fire truck this morning. We have something unexpected for you today too."

Mist stepped out into the lobby and retrieved the violin case that had been hidden behind the registration counter, a red bow wrapped around it. She returned to the front parlor and set it down in front of Camille, whose hands had flown up to cover her mouth. Lauren took a quick photo of her daughter's reaction and then brushed a tear away from her eye. Poppy, having been clued in on the secret, gave Camille a hug.

"How?" Camille glanced around at her parents, Mist, and others, too surprised to expand her sentence.

"We have a friend at the university where Nigel—the professor to most of you—and I both teach," Michael said. "He runs a program collecting instruments from people who donate them and passing them on to others who are looking for them."

"A bit like recycling," the professor said. "A jolly clever idea, really."

Camille turned to her parents. "Did you know about this?"

"Not until we were here," Lauren said. "Mist and Michael suggested it."

"We thought it was a wonderful idea," Keith added. "It's a great program. In fact, I have an old flute I haven't touched for years that I'm going to send them when we get home."

"That dusty case in the closet?" Camille asked.

Keith laughed. "Yes. Now that you put it that way, it makes even more sense. Someone else will be able to use it."

"How about opening it up?" Mist suggested gently.

Camille nodded, took the ribbon off, unhooked the metal latches, and lifted the lid. She gasped at the sight of the violin. "It's beautiful." She looked up. "I don't know how to play it." She announced this as if it had just occurred to her.

"*Yet*," the professor pointed out. "That's rather the point in getting the instrument, my dear."

"We're going to look into getting lessons for you when we get back home," Lauren said.

"Thank you so much!" Camille launched herself into her parents' arms, though not before carefully closing and latching the violin case.

The festivities continued as the hours passed. With no one checking out until the following day, morning moved seamlessly into afternoon and then to evening. Dinner came together so creatively that only the keenest eye could identify it as a reincarnation of the previous night's meal. And even if they did, no one would dare call it by its proper description: leftovers.

To a comforting fire and soft Christmas jazz, guests enjoyed a final night together in the front parlor. Some lingered to discuss their favorite parts of the holiday visit while others turned in early to rest up for early departures.

With gentle nudging from both Michael and Betty, Mist—after restocking beverages and treats in the lobby—left to relax at home, knowing she'd be back early the next morning to set out breakfast and see guests off.

Chapter Seventeen

Mist arrived at the hotel a little before six the next morning to whip up a batch of scones to slide into the oven and to get coffee going for the lobby's beverage counter, which was always set up by six thirty. Clive had offered to scramble or fry eggs to order, and Betty had prepared a fruit platter the night before, a delightful surprise to Mist upon opening the refrigerator. Maisie popped into the kitchen and helped arrange a tray of bacon before taking a seat at a table with Clayton and his parents.

Justine and Randall were first to arrive downstairs for breakfast, depositing suitcases in the lobby on their way into the café. The Coopers soon followed, luggage also in hand. Lauren and Keith took a table of their own and were soon joined by Clara and Andrew. Michael slid in shortly after that.

Ben and Camille sat at a table they dubbed "the cool kids' table," where—by their unofficial rules—Poppy was the only age exception allowed to sit there. Clay Jr, of course, was welcome, and he soon slid into a chair with the others when Clayton and Maisie showed up.

"This was a fabulous holiday," Justine said. "The friends who told us about spending Christmas here said it was wonderful, but we never dreamed it would be this special."

"Memories to last a lifetime," Randall said. This comment warmed Mist's heart, as she believed memories were the best gifts guests could take with them.

"I'm coming back every year to ride with you and your dad," Ben announced to Clay Jr. as he waved a piece of bacon in the air. "You're so lucky to have your very own fire truck."

"I have to share it with the other firemen," Clay Jr said matter-of-factly. He picked up a piece of bacon and challenged Ben to a laser fight, which began and ended just as quickly once Lauren and Maisie noticed the dueling bacon strips. Mist, having watched the bacon skirmish, was reminded to set aside a few strips for a canine treat later on.

The morning moved on, filled with reluctant goodbyes and nostalgic reminiscences serving as parting words. The professor and Poppy left right after breakfast, aiming to get Poppy situated in student housing. Clive left right after the last egg was served in order to open the gallery for after-Christmas sales.

The Coopers and Taylors were soon on the road as well while Clara and Andrew stayed until midafternoon. Parting was not quite as difficult as it was for others since they were yearly visitors and knew time passed quickly—too quickly, Clara noted—and they'd be back the following Christmas.

At the end of the day, when the last dish had been dried and put away, when the front parlor sat empty, when all the guests had departed for destinations near and far, Betty and Mist stood in front of the parlor window. As snowflakes fell gently outside, the lights of the Christmas tree twinkled and soft strains of "Silent Night" embraced them. They exchanged a hug, content that the holiday had been a rousing success. The following year promised to be equally enchanting. Just as the year after that would be. After all, no one familiar with the Timberton Hotel would ever expect anything less.

Betty's Cookie Exchange Recipes

Glazed Cinnamon Nuts
Chocolate-Dipped Orange Butter Cookies
Sugar Cookies
Christmas Popcorn
Rhonda's Fudge
Icebox Fruitcake
Dayna's Oatmeal Cookies
Date Nut Torte Squares
Salted Peanut Cookies
Cranberry White Chocolate Bars
Caramel Apple Cookies
Gluten-Free Chocolate Chip Cookies
Pecan Cheese Wafers
Gingerbread Kiss Cookies
Million Dollar Fudge
Almond Crunch Bars
Pecan Fingers
Momma's Sour Cream Walnuts

Red Velvet Cake Cookies
Cheesecake Stuffed Strawberry Cookies
Graham Cracker Toffee Bars
Wassail

Glazed Cinnamon Nuts

(a family recipe)

Ingredients:

1 cup sugar
1/4 cup water
1/8 teaspoon cream of tartar
Heaping teaspoon of cinnamon
1 tablespoon butter
1-1/2 cups walnut halves

Directions:

Boil sugar, water, cream of tartar, and cinnamon to soft boil stage (236°).

Remove from heat.

Add butter and walnuts.

Stir until walnuts separate. Place on waxed paper to cool.

Chocolate Dipped Orange Butter Cookies

(Submitted by Diane Jewell)

Ingredients:

1 cup (2 sticks) butter, softened
1 cup confectioners' sugar
1 egg
2 1/2 teaspoons Pure Orange Extract
2 1/2 cups sifted flour
1/4 teaspoon salt
6 ounces semi-sweet chocolate, chopped
1 1/2 teaspoons shortening

Directions:

Preheat oven to 350°F. Beat butter and sugar in large bowl with electric mixer on medium speed until light and fluffy. Beat in egg and 1 1/2 teaspoons of the orange extract.

Gradually beat in flour and salt until well mixed. Drop dough by rounded teaspoons onto ungreased baking sheets; flatten with fork.

Bake 12 to 14 minutes or until lightly browned. Cool on baking sheets 1 minute. Remove to wire racks; cool completely.

Melt chocolate and shortening in microwavable bowl on HIGH 1 1/2 minutes, stirring after 30 seconds. Add remaining 1 teaspoon extract; stir until chocolate is completely melted. Dip each cookie halfway into chocolate mixture. Let stand at room temperature or refrigerate on wax paper-lined tray 15 minutes or until chocolate is set.

Sugar Cookies

(Submitted by Rhonda Sowers)

Ingredients:

1 cup powdered sugar
1 cup sugar
1 cup corn oil
1 cup butter
1 teaspoon cream of tarter
2 eggs
1 teaspoon vanilla
4 cups + 1 tablespoon flour
1 teaspoon salt
1 teaspoon baking soda

Directions:

Cream sugars, oil, butter, and vanilla until fluffy.

Beat eggs until light and add creamed mixture.

Add flour and rest of ingredients. Blend well.

Roll into balls. Place on ungreased cookie sheet.

Press flat with glass dipped in sugar.

Bale at 375 degrees or until slightly brown.

Christmas Popcorn

(Submitted by Betty Escobar)

Ingredients:

1/2 cup popcorn kernels
1 bag (12 ounce) vanilla candy melts
1 1/2 cups pretzels, small or broken
1 bag (10 ounces) red and green M&Ms
Red and green holiday sprinkles

Directions:

Pop the popcorn and discard unpopped kernels. Add pretzels and M&Ms.

Melt the candy melts in a microwave safe bowl for 30 seconds at 50% power. Stir and repeat until melted and smooth.

Pour half the melted candy over the popcorn/pretzel mixture and stir.

Drizzle remaining melted candy over the mixture. Do not over stir.

Pour mixture onto wax paper and add sprinkles. Allow to cool.

Break into pieces and store in an airtight container.

Chocolate Candy Cane Fudge
(Submitted by Rhonda Gothier)

Ingredients:
1 bag chocolate chips
1 can condensed milk
Candy canes

Directions:

Melt 1 bag chocolate chips. Add can condensed milk.

Pour in greased foil-lined 9 x 9 pan.

Crush a few candy canes and sprinkle on top.

Refrigerate until solid.

Pull out of pan using foil liner and cut in squares.

Store in airtight container.

Ice Box Fruitcake

(Submitted by Alma Collins)

Ingredients:
- 1 1/2 cups butter
- 1 lb. chopped dates
- 16 oz. small marshmallows
- 1 lb. vanilla wafers, crushed
- 2 teaspoons vanilla
- 4 tablespoons brown sugar
- 1 lb. candied fruit
- 4 cups pecans, chopped
- 2 pkg. coconut

Directions:

Over low heat, melt the butter, dates, and marshmallows. Mix the rest of the ingredients except the coconut in a large bowl.

When the butter, dates, and marshmallow mixture is melted, pour over the other ingredients and mix well.

Pour 1 pkg. coconut on waxed paper. Roll fruitcake into logs (whatever size you prefer) then roll logs in coconut to cover.

Wrap each log in aluminum foil and refrigerate until set. Slice each log into slices.

Dayna's Oatmeal Cookies
(Submitted by Dayna Crandall)

Ingredients:
1 cup shortening
3/4 cup brown sugar
3/4 cup sugar
1 teaspoon vanilla
2 eggs
1/2 teaspoon water
1 1/3 cups flour
2 cups rolled oats
1 teaspoon baking soda
1 teaspoon salt
2 teaspoons cinnamon
2 cups walnuts (optional)
1 large pkg. semi-sweet chocolate chips (optional)

Directions:

Cream sugar and shortening. Beat in vanilla, eggs, and water.

Combine dry ingredients and stir in.

Fold in chips and nuts if desired.

Press balls flat or drop 1 tablespoon-sized onto ungreased baking sheet.

Bake at 375 degrees for 10-12 minutes.

Date Nut Torte Squares
(Submitted by Molly Elliott)

Ingredients:
- 1 cup chopped dates
- 1 cup chopped nuts
- 1 cup sugar
- 2 eggs, beaten
- 2 tablespoons flour
- 1 teaspoon baking powder

Directions:

Mix all ingredients together and bake at 300 degrees for 30 minutes.

Cut into squares and dust with powdered sugar.

Salted Peanut Cookies

(Submitted by Brenda Ellis)

Ingredients:

1 cup shortening

2 cup brown sugar

2 eggs, beaten

2 cups flour

1 teaspoon baking soda

1 teaspoon baking powder

1/2 teaspoon salt

2 cups oatmeal

1 cup Wheaties

1 cup chopped, salted peanuts

Directions:

Cream shortening and sugar. Blend in eggs.

Add sifted dry ingredients.

Add oatmeal, Wheaties, and peanuts.

Drop by teaspoon and flatten with a fork dipped in sugar.

Bake at 350 degrees for approx. 12 minutes or until done.

Cranberry White Chocolate Bars
(Submitted by Molly Elliott)

Ingredients:
2 large eggs
1/2 teaspoon vanilla extract
1 cup sugar
1 cup all-purpose flour
1/4 teaspoon salt
1/2 cup butter, melted
3/4 cups fresh or frozen (thawed) cranberries, coarsely chopped
1/2 (11-oz) bag white chocolate chips

Directions:

Preheat oven to 350 degrees.

Whisk together eggs and vanilla extract in a mixing bowl until blended. Gradually add sugar, beating until blended.

Stir in flour, salt, and melted butter.

Gently stir in cranberries and white chocolate chips.

Spread dough in a lightly greased 8-inch square pan.

Bake 38 to 40 minutes or until a toothpick inserted in center comes out clean.

Cool and cut into bars.

Caramel Apple Cookies

(Submitted by Shelia Hall)

Ingredients:
Cookies:
1/2 cup shortening

1 1/4 cups packed brown sugar

1 egg

1/2 cup apple juice

2 1/4 cups whole wheat pastry flour or all-purpose flour

1 teaspoon baking soda

1 teaspoon ground cinnamon

1/4 teaspoon ground cloves

1/4 teaspoon salt

1 medium tart apple, peeled, cored, and coarsely shredded (1 cup)

3/4 cup golden raisins
Frosting:
2 tablespoon margarine

1/3 cup packed light brown sugar

2 tablespoons water

1 3/4 cups sifted powdered sugar

Fat-free milk

1/3 cup finely chopped walnuts

Directions:

Preheat oven to 350 degrees. Beat shortening and add the 1 1/4 cups brown sugar with an electric mixer on medium speed until combined. Add egg; beat 1 minute. Add apple juice; beat at low speed until blended. Stir together flour, baking soda, cinnamon, cloves, and salt. Add to egg mixture, beating at low speed until combined. Fold in apple and raisins.

Drop dough by slightly rounded teaspoonfuls 1-1/2 inches apart onto ungreased cookie sheet. Bake in preheated oven for 8 minutes or until edges are lightly browned. Let stand 1 minute on cookie sheet. Remove to wire racks and cool.

For the frosting, heat margarine, 1/3 cup brown sugar, and water over medium-high heat, stirring until sugar dissolves. Remove from heat. Stir in sifted powdered sugar. If frosting begins to harden, stir in small amount of fat-free milk to make a spreading consistency. Spread cookies with caramel frosting and sprinkle with walnuts. Makes about 72.

Gluten-Free Chocolate Chip Cookies

(submitted by Petrenia Etheridge)

Ingredients:

2 bananas, mashed
1 cup oats
1/2 cup choc chips
1 teaspoon cinnamon
1 teaspoon vanilla

Directions:

Mix ingredients together and spoon onto parchment paper.

Bake at 350 for 20 min.

Pecan Cheese Wafers
(Submitted by Petrenia Etheridge)

Ingredients:
1 cup shredded cheese
1 stick butter
1/2 cup all-purpose flour
1 cup chopped pecans
1 teaspoon seasoning of choice

Directions:

Cream butter and cheese. Mix seasoning in flour then add to mixture.

Continue mixing as you add in pecans.

Roll into small balls and smash flat.

Bake at 350 for 10-12 minutes.

Gingerbread Kiss Cookies

(Submitted by Kim Davis of *Cinnamon and Sugar and a Little Bit of Murder* blog)

Makes 40 – 45 cookies depending on size

Ingredients:

3/4 cup unsalted butter, room temperature

3/4 cup brown sugar, packed

1/2 cup molasses

1 egg, room temperature

1 teaspoon vanilla extract

3 cups all-purpose flour

2 teaspoon ground ginger

1 teaspoon ground cinnamon

1/2 teaspoon ground nutmeg

1/2 teaspoon allspice

1 teaspoon salt

1 teaspoon baking soda

Coarse sparkling sugar (regular granulated sugar can be substituted)

1 bag chocolate striped Hershey Kisses (regular Hershey Kisses can be substituted), unwrapped

Directions:

In a large bowl, whisk together the flour, ginger, cinnamon, nutmeg, allspice, baking soda, and salt. Set aside.

In the bowl of a stand mixer, beat the brown sugar and butter together until light and fluffy. Add in the molasses, egg, and vanilla extract and beat until well combined.

Slowly add the dry ingredients and mix until incorporated.

Cover with plastic wrap and refrigerate the dough for 30 to 60 minutes.

Preheat oven to 350 degrees (F) and line 2 baking sheets with parchment paper.

Form the chilled dough into small walnut-sized balls. Roll each ball in the coarse sparkling sugar then place on the prepared baking sheets.

Bake for 8 to 10 minutes.

Remove from the oven and place a Hershey Kiss into the center of the cookies. Cool on the baking sheet for 5 minutes then remove to a wire rack to cool completely before serving.

Million Dollar Fudge
(Submitted by Sally Jo Walker)

Ingredients:
12 ounces semisweet chocolate morsels
12 ounces sweet chocolate, broken into small pieces
2 cups marshmallow cream
4 1/2 cups sugar
Pinch salt
2 tablespoons butter
1 1/2 cups (12 ounces) canned evaporated milk
2 cups coarsely chopped nuts (optional)

Directions:

Stir together all chocolate and marshmallow cream.

Bring sugar, salt, butter, and evaporated milk to a boil. Lower heat and simmer 7 minutes.

Pour the hot mixture over the chocolate and marshmallow cream and mix.

Stir in the chopped nuts.

Pour into a greased 9x13 baking dish. Let stand until firm.

Almond Crunch Bars

(Submitted by Betty Escobar)

Ingredients:

1 1/2 cups chocolate chips
1/2 cup almond butter
1/4 teaspoon salt
2 cups rice cereal

Directions:

Melt chocolate chips, almond butter, and salt together, stirring until smooth.

Place rice cereal in a bowl and pour the melted mixture over it. Stir until evenly coated.

Place parchment paper into a greased 9x5 loaf pan. The greased pan will hold the parchment paper in place.

Press the mixture into the loaf pan and smooth the top.

Set in the freezer for 1 hour to firm up.

Lift out with parchment paper and cut into 1-inch bars.

Keep in an airtight container in the fridge for 2 weeks or freeze for up to 3 months.

Pecan Fingers
(Submitted by Shelia Hall)

Ingredients:
6 tablespoons butter
3oz. shortening
3/4 cup confectioners' sugar
1 1/2 cups plain flour
2 eggs
1 cup packed brown sugar
2 tablespoons flour
1/2 teaspoon baking powder
1/2 teaspoon salt
1/2 teaspoon vanilla
1 cup pecans

Directions:

Heat oven to 350 degrees.

Cream together shortening, butter, and confectioners' sugar. Blend in flour.

Press evenly in bottom of a 13x9 ungreased baking pan.

Bake 12-15 minutes. Mix remaining ingredients and spread over hot baked layer.

Return to oven and bake 20 minutes.

Let cool then cut into 3x1 inch bars.

Momma's Sour Cream Walnuts

(Submitted by Lanette Fields)

Ingredients:

1/2 cup of sour cream
1 cup packed dark brown sugar
1/2 cup granulated sugar
1 teaspoon real vanilla
2 1/2 cups of walnut halves

Directions:

Cook first 3 ingredients over medium heat until candy thermometer reaches 236 degrees.

Remove from heat and add vanilla. Beat until mixture starts to thicken.

Add walnuts and stir until well coated.

Turn out onto greased or parchment lined cookie sheet. Break into pieces.

Red Velvet Cake Cookies

(Submitted by Colleen Galster)

Ingredients:

1 box of Red Velvet Cake Mix, any brand

2 large eggs

1/2 cup unsalted butter, melted

1 1/2 cups of your mix in (white chocolate chips are my favorite) or skip these if desired

Cream cheese frosting (if desired) or sprinkles/toppings of choice

Suggestions to mix in:

White Chocolate Chips

Chocolate Chips

Butterscotch Chips

Caramel

Sprinkles

M&Ms

Petite Mints

Directions:

Place cake mix, eggs, and butter in a large bowl. Stir until the batter is smooth. You can do this with a wooden spoon or a hand mixer. Stir in add ins of your choice, if using.

Scoop 2 tablespoon sized cookie dough balls onto cookie sheets lined with parchment paper. Chill for at least one hour.

Preheat oven to 350°F. Bake chilled cookies for about 11-13 minutes, or until the edges just start to get golden brown.

If desired, frost cooled cookies with cream cheese frosting.

Store in an airtight container for up to 3 days or freeze for up to one month.

Cheesecake Stuffed Strawberry Cookies

(Submitted by Nettie Moore from the blog Moore or Less Cooking)

Ingredients:

15 oz strawberry cake mix
1/3 cup of oil
1 teaspoon of vanilla
2 eggs
1 cup of white chocolate chips
1 (8 oz) block of cream cheese
1 teaspoon vanilla
3 tablespoons sugar

Directions:

In a large bowl mix cake mix, oil, vanilla, and eggs and mix with a hand mixer until nice and smooth. Add in white chocolate chips and mix again.

Place bowl in the fridge for 20 minutes.

In a medium-large bowl mix cream cheese, sugar, and vanilla. Mix with a hand mixer until smooth.

Place parchment paper on a tray. Using an ice cream scooper, scoop balls and drop them onto the paper, it should make 12. Place in the freezer for 40 minutes or until the cookie mixture is done.

Place parchment paper down on a large baking sheet. Roll 1 1/2 inch amounts of cookie mixture into balls.

Once all 12 are laid out on paper, place them inside the fridge again for 40 minutes.

Preheat oven to 350 degrees while waiting. Flatten the cookie mixture out, and place 1 cream cheese ball inside it. Roll into a ball using your hands, making sure the cream cheese doesn't leak out.

Once all rolled out, place into the preheated oven for 10-12 minutes.

When done set out to cool and enjoy!

Tips:

If the cookie mixture is too sticky when handling, place it in the fridge for 20 more minutes.

Add more chocolate chips to the outside of the dough balls before placing them into the oven.

Make sure you can't see any cream cheese when you roll it into a ball so it doesn't leak out.

Graham Cracker Toffee Bars

(Submitted by Nettie Moore from the blog Moore or Less Cooking)

Ingredients:

12 graham crackers, broken in half (24 squares in total)
1 stick of butter
3/4 cup of brown sugar
6 ounces semisweet chocolate chips
1 cup chopped pecans

Directions:

Gather all of the ingredients. Pre-heat your oven to 350 degrees.

Get a 12x18 sheet pan and line it with foil and spray with non-stick spray.

Arrange graham crackers in a square. (Make sure they are touching.)

In a saucepan, bring butter and brown sugar to a boil on medium heat. Cook for two minutes while stirring constantly until melted and bubbly.

Immediately pour over graham crackers and spread evenly.

Bake in the oven for approx. 6 minutes, until light brown and bubbly.

Sprinkle chocolate chips all over the crackers, then bake again for 2 minutes.

Take out of the oven and spread the chocolate chips over the crackers.

Sprinkle with pecans. Lightly press the pecans down into the chocolate.

Cool completely and break into squares.

Tips and Tricks:

Instead of pecans, use pretzels or peanuts.
    Add extra chocolate chips if you like it a little more on the chocolate side.
    You can use dark chocolate instead of milk chocolate!

Wassail

(Submitted by Elizabeth Christy with gratitude to Patricia Christy)

Ingredients:

2 quarts apple cider
1/2 cup sugar
1/4 cup firmly packed brown sugar
2 cinnamon sticks
12 whole cloves
4 cups of grapefruit juice
4 cups of orange juice
1 cup of pineapple juice

Directions:

Combine the apple cider, sugar, brown sugar, cinnamon sticks, and cloves and bring to a boil.

Cook until the sugar dissolves. Reduce heat and simmer for 5 minutes.

Add the grapefruit, orange, and pineapple juices.

Heat until hot, but do not boil. Strain out the chunks.

May be refrigerated and reheated as needed or wanted.

Recipe Notes

Recipe Notes

Recipe Notes

Recipe Notes

Acknowledgments

It is because of the efforts of many that *Evergreen Wishes at Moonglow* exists. I'm grateful for Annie Sarac's fantastic editing and guidance. Her expertise helped make this book shine. I owe heartfelt thanks to Elizabeth Christy for nudging me through a smattering of developmental roadblocks along the way. Jay Garner, Karen Putnam, Carol Anderson, and Paul Sterrett all helped with beta reading and plot feedback. Mariah Sinclair's amazing graphic design talent is what brought the beautiful cover to life. And the Georgetown Writers deserve kudos for their constant support and encouragement.

Christmas at the Timberton Hotel wouldn't be the same without Betty's annual cookie exchange. The delicious recipes in this year's book are thanks to Kim Davis and her blog, *Cinnamon and Sugar and a Little Bit of Murder*, Nettie Moore and her blog, *Moore or Less Cooking*, Petrenia Etheridge, Shelia Hall, Lanette Fields, Betty Escobar, Colleen Galster, Diane Jewell, Rhonda Sowers, Rhonda Gothier, Alma Collins, Dayna Crandall, Brenda Ellis, Sally Jo Walker, and Elizabeth Christy. Go on now. Preheat that oven and get baking!

Books by Deborah Garner

The Paige MacKenzie Series

Above the Bridge

When NY reporter Paige MacKenzie arrives in Jackson Hole, it's not long before her instincts tell her there's more than a basic story to be found in the popular, northwestern Wyoming mountain area. A chance encounter with attractive cowboy Jake Norris soon has Paige chasing a legend of buried treasure passed down through generations. Sidestepping a few shady characters who are also searching for the same hidden reward, she will have to decide who is trustworthy and who is not.

The Moonglow Café

The discovery of an old diary inside the wall of the historic hotel soon sends NY reporter Paige MacKenzie into the underworld of art and deception. Each of the town's residents holds a key to untangling more than one long-buried secret, from the hippie chick owner of a new age café to the mute homeless man in the town park. As the worlds of western art and sapphire mining collide, Paige finds herself juggling research, romance, and danger.

Three Silver Doves

The New Mexico resort of Agua Encantada seems a perfect destination for reporter Paige MacKenzie to combine work with well-deserved rest and relaxation. But when suspicious jewelry shows up on another guest, and the town's storyteller goes missing, Paige's R&R is soon redefined as restlessness and risk. Will an unexpected overnight trip to Tierra Roja Casino lead her to the answers she seeks, or are darker secrets lurking along the way?

Hutchins Creek Cache

When a mysterious 1920s coin is discovered behind the Hutchins Creek Railroad Museum in Colorado, Paige MacKenzie starts digging into four generations of Hutchins family history, with a little help from the Denver Mint. As legends of steam engines and coin mintage mingle, will Paige discover the true origin of the coin, or will she find herself riding the rails dangerously close to more than one long-hidden town secret?

Crazy Fox Ranch

As Paige MacKenzie returns to Jackson Hole, she has only two things on her mind: enjoy life with Wyoming's breathtaking Grand Tetons as the backdrop and spend more time with handsome cowboy Jake Norris as he prepares to open his guest ranch. But when a stranger's odd behavior leads her to research Western filming in the area—in particular, the movie *Shane*, will it simply lead to a freelance article for the *Manhattan Post*, or will it lead to a dangerous, hidden secret?

Sweet Sierra Gulch

Paige MacKenzie isn't convinced there's anything "sweet" about Sweet Sierra Gulch when she arrives in the small California Gold Rush town. Still, there's plenty of history as well as anticipated romance with her favorite cowboy, Jake Norris. But when the owner of the local café goes missing, Paige is determined to find out why. Will she uncover a dangerous secret in the town's old mining tunnels, or will curiosity land her in over her head?

The Sadie Kramer Flair Series

A Flair for Chardonnay

When flamboyant senior sleuth Sadie Kramer learns the owner of her favorite chocolate shop is in trouble, she heads for the California wine country with a tote-bagged Yorkie and a slew of questions. The fourth generation Tremiato Winery promises answers, but not before a dead body turns up at the vintners' scheduled Harvest Festival. As Sadie juggles truffles, tips, and turmoil, she'll need to sort the grapes from the wrath in order to find the identity of the killer.

A Flair for Drama

When a former schoolmate invites Sadie Kramer to a theatre production, she jumps at the excuse to visit the Monterey Bay area for a weekend. Plenty of action is expected on stage, but when the show's leading lady turns up dead, Sadie finds herself faced with more than one drama to follow. With both cast members and production crew as potential suspects, will Sadie and her sidekick Yorkie, Coco, be able to solve the case?

A Flair for Beignets

With fabulous music, exquisite cuisine, and rich culture, how could a week in New Orleans be anything less than fantastic for Sadie Kramer and her sidekick Yorkie, Coco? And it is... until a customer at a popular patisserie drops dead face-first in a raspberry-almond tart. A competitive bakery, a newly formed friendship, and even her hotel's luxurious accommodations offer possible suspects. As Sadie sorts through a gumbo of interconnected characters, will she discover who the killer is, or will the killer discover her first?

A Flair for Truffles

Sadie Kramer's friendly offer to deliver three boxes of gourmet Valentine's Day truffles for her neighbor's chocolate shop backfires when she arrives to find the intended recipient deceased. Even more intriguing is the fact that the elegant heart-shaped gifts were ordered by three different men. With the help of one detective and the hindrance of another, Sadie will search San Francisco for clues. But will she find out "whodunit" before the killer finds a way to stop her?

A Flair for Flip-Flops

When the body of a heartthrob celebrity washes up on the beach outside Sadie Kramer's luxury hotel suite, her fun in the sun soon turns into sleuthing with the stars. The resort's wine and appetizer gatherings, suspicious guest behavior, and casual strolls along the beach boardwalk may provide clues, but will they be enough to discover who the killer is, or will mystery and mayhem leave a Hollywood scandal unsolved?

A Flair for Goblins

When Sadie Kramer agrees to help decorate for San Francisco's high-society Halloween shindig, she expects to find whimsical ghosts, skeletons, and jack-o-lanterns when she shows up at the Wainwright Mansion—not a body. With two detectives, a paranormal investigator turned television star, and a cauldron full of family members cackling around her, Sadie and her sidekick Yorkie are determined to find out who the killer is. Will an old superstition help lead to the truth? Or will this simply become one more tale in the mansion's haunted history?

A Flair for Shamrocks

When flamboyant senior sleuth Sadie Kramer's car breaks down outside a small Oregon beach town, the repair lands her in unexpected lodging above an Irish pub for St. Patrick's Day. With pub games, green beer, and a potbellied pig named Paddy in the mix, it's bound to be a unique holiday. But not all is what it seems in Irishton, especially when the owner of the pub turns up dead. An assortment of local characters could be guilty, but only one is the killer. Sadie and her sidekick Yorkie will need the luck of the Irish to solve the mystery.

The Moonglow Christmas Series

Mistletoe at Moonglow

The small town of Timberton, Montana, hasn't been the same since resident chef and artist, Mist, arrived, bringing a unique new age flavor to the old western town. When guests check in for the holidays, they bring along worries, fears, and broken hearts, unaware that Mist has a way of working magic in people's lives. One thing is certain: no matter how cold winter's grip is on each guest, no one leaves Timberton without a warmer heart.

Silver Bells at Moonglow

Christmas brings an eclectic gathering of visitors and locals to the Timberton Hotel each year, guaranteeing an eventful season. Add in a hint of romance, and there's more than snow in the air around the small Montana town. When the last note of Christmas carols has faded away, the soft whisper of silver bells from the front door's wreath will usher guests and townsfolk back into the world with hope for the coming year.

Gingerbread at Moonglow

The Timberton Hotel boasts an ambiance of near-magical proportions during the Christmas season. As the aromas of ginger, cinnamon, nutmeg, and molasses mix with heartfelt camaraderie and sweet romance, holiday guests share reflections on family, friendship, and life. Will decorating the outside of a gingerbread house prove easier than deciding what goes inside?

Nutcracker Sweets at Moonglow

When a nearby theater burns down just before Christmas, cast members of *The Nutcracker* arrive at the Timberton Hotel with only a sliver of holiday joy. Camaraderie, compassion, and shared inspiration combine to help at least one hidden dream come true. As with every Christmas season, this year's guests will face the New Year with a renewed sense of hope.

Snowfall at Moonglow

As holiday guests arrive at the Timberton Hotel with hopes of a white Christmas, unseasonably warm weather hints at a less-than-wintery wonderland. But whether the snow falls or not, one thing is certain: with resident artist and chef, Mist, around, there's bound to be a little magic. No one ever leaves Timberton without renewed hope for the future.

Yuletide at Moonglow

When a Yuletide festival promises jovial crowds, resident artist and chef, Mist, knows she'll have her hands full. Between the legendary Christmas Eve dinner at the Timberton Hotel and this season's festival events, the unique magic of Christmas in this small Montana town offers joy, peace, and community to guests and townsfolk alike. As always, no one will return home without a renewed sense of hope for the future.

Starlight at Moonglow

As the Christmas holiday approaches, a blizzard threatens the peaceful ambiance that the Timberton Hotel usually offers its guests. Even resident artist and chef, Mist, known to work near miracles, has no control over the howling winds and heavy snowfall. But there's always a bit of magic in this small Montana town, and this year's storm may just find it's no match for heartfelt camaraderie, joyful inspiration, and sweet romance.

Joy at Moonglow

Each holiday season is unique in the small Montana town of Timberton. New and returning guests bring their dreams, cares, and worries, and always leave with lighter hearts and renewed hope for the future. But no season has ever been as special as this one. Because, to everyone's delight, wedding bells will be ringing. Thanks to the heartfelt efforts of many and no shortage of sweet romance, this year will be the most joyful of all.

Evergreen Wishes at Moonglow

Christmas in the small town of Timberton, Montana, is always filled with holiday traditions, exquisite cuisine, and heartfelt camaraderie. When a majestic evergreen tree is placed in the center of town, inviting ornaments containing wishes, townsfolk and visitors are soon pondering what their hopes and dreams might be. Although wishes can't always come true, some just might with a bit of holiday magic.

Additional titles:

Cranberry Bluff

Molly Elliott's quiet life is disrupted when routine errands land her in the middle of a bank robbery. Accused and cleared of the crime, she flees both media attention and mysterious, threatening notes to run a bed-and-breakfast on the Northern California coast. Her new beginning is peaceful until five guests show up at the inn, each with a hidden agenda. As true motives become apparent, will Molly's past come back to haunt her, or will she finally be able to leave it behind?

Sweet Treats: Recipes from the Moonglow Christmas Series

Delicious recipes, including Glazed Cinnamon Nuts, Cherry Pecan Holiday Cookies, Chocolate Peppermint Bark, Cranberry Drop Cookies, White Christmas Fudge, Molasses Sugar Cookies, Lemon Crinkles, Spiced Apple Cookies, Swedish Coconut Cookies, Double-Chocolate Walnut Brownies, Blueberry Oatmeal Cookies, Cocoa Kisses, Angel Crisp Cookies, Gingerbread Eggnog Trifle, Dutch Sour Cream Cookies, and more!

For more information on Deborah Garner's books:

Facebook: https://www.facebook.com/deborahgarnerauthor

Twitter: https://twitter.com/PaigeandJake

Website: http://deborahgarner.com

Mailing list: http://bit.ly/deborahgarner

www.ingramcontent.com/pod-product-compliance
Lightning Source LLC
Chambersburg PA
CBHW030828200726
48285CB00007B/2395